NIGHT SHOOT

DAVID SODERGREN

D1617770

Cover art and illustrations by Connor Leslie
Graphic design by Heather Sodergren

To Boris,
For sitting still long enough to let me write.

1

He was late.

My God. *My God!*

He was late, and so he ran, the ruin of his car far behind him now, curled around a pine tree and belching black smoke into the atmosphere. He shouldn't have been driving so fast, not at night, not when it was raining, but he was going to be *late*, dammit. Late!

Branches whipped across his face as he hurtled through the ancient forest. He chanced a glance at his watch and saw it was almost eight.

You'll never make it, he thought, silently cursing himself. *You're too damn late.*

The woods were dark, impenetrable to most, but he knew where he was headed. His foot caught a root and he crashed to the forest bed. Scrambling to his feet, he spat out a mouthful of pine needles and continued his mad dash, ignoring the pain that flared through his arm, his heart pumping. The forest was his only chance, a shortcut. The road was safer, but tonight safety took a backseat to punctuality. It had to.

It simply *had* to.

A light flickered in the distance, faint at first, then growing brighter. Nearly there! The trees parted and he was out, free from the grasping branches that tugged and tore at his suit, free from the claustrophobic forest he had spent his childhood exploring. His feet skipped over the grass, kicking up dirt as he raced towards the building.

Crawford Manor.

It had stood for centuries, a brooding sentinel overlooking the North Sea, long enough for old mysteries to settle and gnarled roots to creep insidiously into the earth. Within the dank walls of Crawford Manor, secrets were given time to breathe.

To atrophy.

To fester.

He knew this all too well.

Another light went on, then another, all across the manor, and a great pit opened in his stomach.

From inside, the grandfather clock tolled eight, the melancholy chimes bleeding through the walls and echoing throughout the clearing.

It was time.

Rummaging in his pocket as he bounded across the lawn, he drew out a set of keys, readying the large rusted one without even looking. He took the steps two at a time, *three* at a time. His shoulder hit the door and the key found the lock, turning fast, and then he was inside, making sure to slam the door behind him. He paused a moment, listening, hearing nothing but the waves crashing against the shore and the *thump-thump* of his heartbeat. Then he heard the scream.

As ever, the sing-song voice in his head mocked him.

Late, late, late. Always, always late.

He lurched forward on unsteady legs, leaving a trail of muddy bootprints across the expensive carpets, the screams *(tortured, horrified)* ringing in his ears, and he knew he would hear them forever more.

'Please,' he croaked. 'I beg you...'

He headed for the dining room, the ungodly shrieks gaining in pitch, piercing his eardrums like hot needles. He stumbled, unable to continue, yet forcing himself to his feet. He had to see.

He had to know.

The door was closed. He faced it the way a boxer would an opponent, except now the fight had left him. His body sagged in defeat.

Late, late, late. Always, always late.

'Shut up! Shut up!' he raged.

The screams stopped.

'Lord in Heaven, forgive me,' he whispered, then turned the handle and let the door swing open. The lights were off and his trembling hand searched for the switch, found it, flicked it, and bathed the room in a sickly orange glow.

'My God,' he said, shaking his head and slumping against the wall, sinking to the floor. His hand shot to his mouth as his vacant eyes darted around the room. He wept.

'My...God.'

He was late.

He was very late indeed.

2

Elspeth Murray awoke in the greatest possible way — to the sound of Kermit the Frog gently crooning *Rainbow Connection* in her ear.

'Shhh, frog,' she whispered, eyelids either half-open or half-closed, it was hard to say.

'That's your alarm,' groaned Sandy Beaumont from the other side of the bed, her eyes *definitely* shut, and that was the way they would stay, thank you very much. As Kermit reached the chorus, Sandy rolled over and nudged Elspeth with her foot. 'Get up. Get up. Get up.'

The pressure was too great, and Elspeth caved. 'Fine,' she grumbled, grabbing her phone and rudely interrupting Kermit's ballad. It was a poor choice of alarm anyway. Too relaxing. She always considered changing it to a song she hated, to give her more incentive to switch it off, but the thought of waking up to Coldplay was unbearable.

The room was pitch black, no morning light peeking

through the blinds into the small flat the two girls shared. Elspeth shuffled from under the duvet and sat on the edge, wondering why it was so dark, and why was the heating not on, and what day was it, and — she glanced at her phone — why the fuck was her alarm going off at 5am?

'Damn you, Kermit,' she whispered, still lost in the delirium of a waking dream.

'Get up,' grumbled Sandy. 'You've got to pick up Deek.'

The shoot! Elspeth wiped the sleep from her eyes. Yup, today was the first day of shooting their final student movie. She had to be at Deek's for six and on location by seven-thirty. That left a full hour to shower and eat breakfast. Elspeth snuggled back under the covers and put her arm around Sandy's waist.

'Get up,' said Sandy, sounding like a broken toy.

Squeeze her waist and she says her famous catchphrase — *Get up!*

Elspeth slid out of bed and lazily searched for her slippers on the cold wooden floor.

'I made you a packed lunch. And your bag's by the door.'

'You're turning into my mum.'

Sandy twisted onto her back. 'You just made it weird,' she said, as Elspeth fumbled around in the sock drawer. 'Oh, and don't worry about the noise, Ellie, I was already awake.'

'Sorry,' laughed Elspeth, not sorry in the slightest. 'Guess you won't mind if I put the light on then?' She hit the switch before Sandy had a chance to respond.

'I hate you.'

'You love me.'

'That too.'

She showered, and when she finished Sandy was sitting in bed reading the script.

'Oh, don't,' groaned Elspeth, trying to snatch it out of Sandy's hands.

'But it's so *good*,' said Sandy. 'I can't wait to see' — she checked the title on the cover page — '*The Haunting of Lacey Carmichael*, by Robert...*Cawford*? Oh my god Ellie, he can't even spell his own name.'

'I don't want to know.'

'This is it, Ellie. This is gonna be your big break, I can feel it.'

'Don't be facetious,' laughed Elspeth. 'It's not attractive.'

Once again Elspeth tried to grab the script but Sandy leapt out of bed, reading aloud now as she ran round the bed in her pyjamas, Elspeth in hot pursuit.

'*Lacey strips and we see her breasts. There is a spooky noise, and she goes to the window and looks out, her breasts pressed up against the glass.*'

Elspeth chased after her. 'Stop it!'

Sandy evaded Elspeth's grasp and jumped back onto the bed, leafing through the pages until she found another 'good bit'. It didn't take long.

'*Lacey is naked. She admires herself in the mirror, plays with her breasts. Then Rex comes in. He is not naked, but they have sex. It's very sexy.*' At that line, Sandy doubled over with laughter.

Elspeth followed Sandy onto the bed and tackled her, forcing her down and lying atop her. She wrestled the script out of her laughing girlfriend's hand.

Sandy giggled. 'It's worse than I imagined! You can't show this film in uni.'

Elspeth laughed too. She was helpless not to. 'I didn't write it!' she grinned, pinning Sandy down.

'You sure? It reads like your wildest fantasies.'

'My only fantasy is you shutting up.' She placed one

hand over Sandy's mouth, the other sneaking up her pyjama top and tickling her. Sandy screamed and fought, but Elspeth was stronger. After enough torture had been dished out, she let her go. Sandy pouted, her face flushed.

'You're horrible.'

'I thought you said you loved me?'

'Not anymore. Shouldn't you be away? This masterpiece isn't going to make itself, and I want to go back to sleep.'

Elspeth rolled off Sandy and lay next to her. The bed was so warm, so comfortable. She never wanted to leave it. But she had to. Her fourth year dissertation was already complete, and this shoot was all that stood between her and a Bachelor's Degree in Film and Photography.

'Yeah, I'd better go. Duty calls. Unless you want me to stay a few minutes longer...'

Elspeth spider-walked her fingers up Sandy's thigh.

'I'll still be here when you get back,' said Sandy. 'Now go, and make sure Robert doesn't exploit the actress, okay? You know what that sleaze bag is like.'

Elspeth rolled her eyes, kissed Sandy on the lips and smiled. 'Don't worry,' she said, grabbing her packed lunch and bag and heading for the door. 'I'll keep him in line.'

She left the flat, blissfully unaware of the nightmare that awaited her.

Things would never be the same again.

Two hours later, Elspeth navigated the narrow track in her Fiat 500, mindful of the steep drop that separated the road from the forest. Tall pines swayed in the morning wind as the wheels of the Fiat scratched over loose gravel. She had taken the turnoff from the main road six miles back and figured she should arrive at her destination soon. So far there had been no sign of Crawford Manor, just endless trees blurring past and the occasional deer staring at her through startled eyes.

The car hit a pothole and, in the passenger seat, Deek Gareth stirred. He had slept for most of the ninety-minute journey from Aberdeen, which wasn't bad going for an adult. Was Deek an adult? Elspeth decided she was feeling charitable, so sure, why not? He had recently shaved his head in a bid to stop getting ID'd when buying booze, but he still looked younger than his twenty-one years. With his round face and puppy fat, he resembled a comically over-sized baby. In comparison, Elspeth thought she looked like a withered old hag. But hey, who looks their best at seven-thirty in the morning, especially if they've been up since five?

Deek's snoring grated on her nerves, so she turned up the volume on the radio, but not even Spandau Ballet's *Gold* could rouse the slumbering boy.

She drove on through the fine morning mist. The rest of the crew would be there already, Robert pacing back and forth with a cigarette and a curse on his lips. Well, Deek could take the blame for that. *She* had been waiting outside at quarter-to-six, exactly as planned. It was Deek who had still been in bed. She had to buzz his flat and cop an earful of abuse from his mum while waiting for Deek to trundle down the stairs and collapse into the car, before drifting back into the welcoming arms of sleep, leaving Elspeth to enjoy or endure the entire journey unencumbered by conversation.

The sky was an angry grey and water dripped from the pine needles of the trees. It was going to be another rotten, stormy Scottish day. She wondered how many exterior shots Robert had planned.

'Are we there yet?' murmured Deek, his eyelids flickering like moths.

'It's alive!'

Deek rested his head on his shoulder and a thin trickle of fluid dribbled down his chin. 'I'm tired.'

'Well, we're almost there,' she said, sounding like his mother, though having now met the woman in question, she wasn't sure which of them she felt most sorry for.

'All I can see is trees.'

'Can't see the forest for the trees, huh?'

'What?'

'Doesn't matter,' smiled Elspeth. 'Try to wake up. Should only be another mile or so.'

Deek rubbed his bleary eyes and stretched, his hands hitting the roof of the car. 'Robert said it's massive. A proper mansion, like Downton Abbey or some shite.'

'Never figured you for a Downton fan.'

Deek made a face. 'My ma watches it.'

'Aye, sure.'

They fell into the comfortable silence of old friends. Well, that or Deek was asleep again. Regardless, they continued down the track, until the forest abruptly ended and Crawford Manor revealed itself in all its ageing, decrepit splendour, the trees deferring to the structure like peasants kneeling before a nobleman. It was about as remote a place as Elspeth could imagine on the Scottish mainland, surrounded on one side by thick woodland, and on the other by the sea. As she carefully steered the vehicle over the rough terrain, she felt like they were driving back in time, the forest a portal to a bygone era. She half-expected to see horse-drawn carriages wheeling through the fog, lit only by the flickering flame of an oil lamp, Jack the Ripper scurrying through the shadows, blood-stained knife in hand.

It was enormous, a sprawling gothic mansion in the middle of nowhere that would surely outlive them all.

Now there's a lovely thought for a cold November morning.

Elspeth smiled.

Deek finally noticed Crawford Manor and sat up, his jaw slack.

'That's an absolute fucking unit.'

'Sure is,' said Elspeth. Crawford Manor *was* an absolute fucking unit, the sort of place her parents would take her to visit on the weekends when she was a kid, a stately home for rich weirdos. To think it belonged to a relative of someone she knew, someone she called a friend, blew her mind. She had grown up in a council flat on one of Edinburgh's roughest estates. Every morning she had to watch her step in case she stood on a discarded needle or a sleeping junkie. Even now, at twenty-five years old, she was unaccustomed to such displays of wealth.

They drove past decrepit stables and a coach-house, a faded KEEP OUT sign nailed over the entrance, the buildings having long ago fallen prey to that most deadly of tenants; neglect. Broken planks jutted from the roof like splintered bones, a thick carpet of moss coating the walls. Elspeth didn't think the sign was necessary. You'd have to be an idiot to go exploring in those condemned death-traps. On second thoughts, there were plenty of idiots out there. Hell, there was one in the car with her. A nice idiot, but an idiot nonetheless.

'Oi, be careful,' yawned Deek as the Fiat shuddered over a bump, his black sports bag rattling in the back seat, hundreds of pounds of borrowed audio recording equipment safely ensconced inside.

'I'm trying to be,' she said.

There wasn't much she could do about it. To call the dirt track a road would be an insult to roads, and it had been like this since the turnoff five or six miles ago. She looked at the fat clouds in the greying sky, hoping the rain wouldn't be too bad. Her poor Fiat would never cope with the mud if a storm hit.

They left the small buildings behind, the mist gobbling them up, then took a hairpin bend and headed for the manor. Several cars were already parked, and she recognised all but one.

'I can't believe we've got this place,' said Elspeth, more to herself than to Deek.

He nodded. 'Robert's family's loaded, like. He probably grew up in a house like this. Fuckin' Monarch of the Glen.'

'It's beautiful.'

Deek whistled. 'Posh as fuck.'

'Yeah, that too,' grinned Elspeth.

She pulled in beside the white rental van. Aiden Jones, their resident camera operator, was in the driver's seat, and he gave them a thumbs-up through the rain-speckled window. Elspeth nodded back and left the car. The air was brisk and shot through with an electrifying chill that nibbled at her fingers. Aiden and Deek soon followed.

'Morning,' said Aiden sleepily, pulling a woollen cap over his forehead.

'Hi Aiden,' she said, her attention drawn to the enormous building. Aiden gave Deek a perfunctory nod and said, 'Awright?'

'Awright,' replied Deek.

It was fascinating stuff, but Elspeth decided to forego

listening to any more of their sparkling repartee and headed off towards the manor, their filming location for the day. And what a location it was! Robert had outdone himself this time. He may be a terrible director, but he was one hell of a location scout. Crawford Manor would, at the very least, give them a heck of a lot of production value, and make Elspeth's job as set dresser that little bit easier. It towered across the skyline, and Elspeth noticed just how close it sat to the edge of the cliff-face. Despite a mild fear of heights, she walked towards the cliff, to where the ground dropped away and the waves of the North Sea crashed relentlessly against the rocks hundreds of feet below. Her stomach lurched.

Too high. *Way* too high.

She stepped back, looking up towards the roof, at the turrets and balustrades, at the carved figurines and gargoyles that decorated the walls. Yup, this would do nicely. Very nicely indeed.

'Elspeth, come on,' shouted Deek. 'Robert will be waiting.'

'Okay, just coming.'

She stood a moment longer in the brooding shadow of Crawford Manor, staring out to sea. It felt like she was standing on the edge of the world, the last woman on Earth. The wind howled, masking the squawks of nesting gulls, and she realised that a particularly strong breeze could lift her off her feet and send her careening over the edge. She backed up further, then walked around the building, tracing her fingers along the rough stone. Deek and Aiden were unpacking, carting heavy equipment from the van into the house. Cameras, tripods, a dolly and track. Deek struggled with his bag, a boom mic balancing precariously on top, while Aiden lugged a flight-case full of spotlights, stopping every ten feet or so to catch his breath and give his arms a rest. Elspeth figured Robert would be inside already, sitting somewhere comfortable and going over the script with Laura, their producer and — most importantly — Robert's girlfriend.

The rising sun glinted off the windows and for the first time Elspeth spotted the bars that adorned the glass panes, thick black wrought-iron ones that covered every window in the house from top to bottom.

Fair enough. There was probably a shit-load of expensive old-person crap in there. Can't have anyone breaking in.

Or out.

Ha! She could feel herself getting in the mood already. She smiled and rubbed her cold hands together, wishing she'd brought her gloves.

Robert had really come through for them.

Crawford Manor was the perfect location for a horror film.

Almost *too* perfect.

3

Robert Crawford watched his crew from behind the barred window like a prisoner in a first-class cell, his fingers tapping nervously on the mantelpiece.

'Lazy bums.'

'What did you say?' asked Laura Gray, highlighting a line in the script and looking up at him. He shook his head and turned to her, adopting the appropriate tone of gravitas.

'My crew has two speeds, Laura. Dead slow and stop. We've got one day here, one day to shoot half of the fucking script, and they're out there dawdling like they're at a church picnic.'

'You could always help?' said Laura, and the pair laughed at the absurdity of the suggestion. Robert settled himself onto the sofa next to Laura and draped an arm over her.

He looked at the heavily annotated script. 'Think we can do it?'

'It'll be tough, but yeah, I think so. If we could just get another hour...'

Robert snorted. 'No chance. We're lucky to even get

today.' He lowered his voice. 'Uncle Ross is the black sheep of the family, a total recluse. He never has anyone round, never turns up to any family events...my dad has to phone him every few months to make sure he's still alive. I think dad secretly hopes that one time, he won't answer. Then this whole place is ours.' He squeezed Laura's shoulder. 'Who knows, maybe one day me and you can live here.'

Laura's eyes sparkled. That was an idea she could get used to.

'So what happened, your dad have compromising photos of him or something?'

Robert grinned. 'Dunno. He said he called in an old favour, whatever that means. Got us one measly day, but it's better than nothing.'

'And we *have* to be out by eight?'

'On the dot. That's when Uncle Ross leaves too.'

Laura looked at him. 'What do you mean?'

Robert stood, heading back to the window. He heard the crunch of frozen grass beneath Deek's feet as he shambled from Elspeth's car, lugging his black sports bag. They were late, putting them behind schedule already. The actors had arrived with Aiden twenty minutes ago and should have been in costume and ready to go by now, costumes that were currently sitting in the trunk of Elspeth's Fiat. He saw Elspeth too, dawdling along, staring at the building in wonder.

Hurry up!

'I asked you a question.'

'Huh?' Robert looked over at his girlfriend and tried to remember what Laura had said. 'Oh, right. Well, my uncle doesn't live here, he just owns it. He has a place in town, apparently. Comes here during the day, goes somewhere else to sleep.'

'Why?'

'Who knows? I guess I come from a long line of great British eccentrics.'

Laura nodded. 'Maybe there're too many bad memories here.'

But Robert wasn't listening. He put his head against the glass and stared out between the bars, his breath fogging the window as he scratched at his beard, pinching the coarse bristles. It was a familiar ritual. At the beginning of every university film project, he stopped shaving and only resumed once the final edit was locked. Laura hated it, complained about the way it chafed her neck and mouth, but she put up with it. She put up with a lot.

'Go check on the actors,' he said. 'Make sure they know their lines. And get everyone to meet me in the hall in ten minutes.'

Annoyed, Laura shuffled her papers and laid them on the grand oak table.

'Time for a rousing speech, is it?'

'Something like that, yeah.' Without another word he left, brushing past her and heading down the hall towards the staircase, taking a right before he reached it and facing another corridor. Like the rest, it was lined with doors and paintings. That was Crawford Manor in a nutshell; doors and paintings, doors and paintings, as far as the eye could see, a mind-bending labyrinth from out of an old Hammer Horror picture.

He stopped outside one of the doors and rapped his knuckles on the wood. His mouth was dry. What was it about Uncle Ross that made him so anxious? He was family, for crying out loud. He knocked again and heard the muffled sound of a deadbolt sliding, then a key unlocking, then another bolt.

Paranoid much?

The door opened a crack, revealing a single eye, lined with wrinkles.

Robert's uncle, Ross Crawford, just stared at him.

'Uh, sir? May I speak with you?'

Crawford's stony expression never wavered.

When Robert was fifteen, he had gone through a goth phase. Black eyeliner, nail varnish, The Sisters of Mercy on repeat. His mother used to say, '*If you smiled, your face would crack.*' He thought of that now, staring at his uncle. The old man sighed.

'What are we doing if not speaking right now?'

'Uh, I suppose. May I come in?'

'Certainly not.'

'Oh,' replied Robert dumbly, already on the back foot.

'I believe I have made my wishes regarding your presence here rather clear. I have granted you access to the upper floor. You may use any room that is unlocked, and you must vacate the premises by eight o'clock. All I ask in return is that you leave the house unmolested, and myself undisturbed. Is this not the case?'

'Yes sir.'

'So why, my dear nephew,' said Crawford, spitting out the words like venom, 'are we currently engaged in this tête-à-tête, delightful as it may be?'

Flustered, Robert looked around for help, wishing he had brought Laura along with him. She was better at communicating. Robert considered himself an artist, his sensitive brain on a different wavelength to normal people. Not that Uncle Ross was normal. Anything but, in fact.

'I just wondered...could we have more time? One more day? You see, we've got a lot of work to do and—'

'I don't need any sob stories. You have one day, correct?'

'Yes sir.'

'And today is that day, correct?'

Robert sighed. 'Yes sir.'

'Now I'm no mathematician — English was always my strong suit — but I do believe your *precious* time, and my own, is being wasted.'

Robert could feel his temperature rising. He hated being spoken down to. He went to his usual last resort.

'I can pay you. I mean, not right now, I don't have cash on me, but I could get it for tomorrow.'

A smell caught in Robert's nostrils, something like spoiled meat. It must have showed on his face, as Crawford opened the door wider and stepped out into the hall, closing it behind him. He stood a good three or four inches taller than Robert, and despite his age — Robert figured him for his mid-seventies — he was a surprisingly intimidating physical presence.

'Take a look around, son. You reckon I'm short of a bob or two? Do I not have enough Persian rugs? Do you stroll around my abode thinking *my*, what a delightful living space, if only there were more expensive and useless antiquities cluttering up the shelves? Or perhaps you believe Crawford Manor is not quite big enough for one family, and it requires an extension to the west wing, or the addition of a conservatory?'

'A family, sir?'

'I said *man*, you foolish boy, not family. Remove the lumpen wax from your ears before engaging with an *adult* in an *adult* conversation. Now, kindly answer my question.'

'Uh, which one, sir?'

Crawford eyeballed him. 'I said, do I look like I need any more money? And don't keep me waiting this time, I'm already giddy with excitement.'

Robert ran a hand through his tousled hair, trying not to let the sarcasm get to him. He looked around the hall, though he needn't have bothered. Everything in the house was expensive, from the furniture to the curtains to the priceless antiques and heirlooms that lined the walls and mantels.

'No sir,' he said.

'Very good. You are here for one simple reason — your father is under the impression I owe him a favour. I suppose in a way he is correct. A fine memory your father has. Regretfully fine. Now, I trust all of your equipment shall be removed from my home by eight o'clock *sharp*?'

'Yeah, sure. It'll be gone.'

'Good.' Mr Crawford smiled. His face didn't crack, but it wasn't exactly heart-warming either. 'Now leave me in peace. I have business to attend to, and it may take some time.' He turned and slithered through the gap in the door, the rotten smell briefly escaping before the door slammed shut in Robert's face. The bolts clicked back into place and the key rattled in the lock.

'Fuck you,' Robert whispered. 'One day, this'll all be mine, and you'll be dead and in your grave.'

Then he strode down the hall to his crew, trying to focus.

He had a film to make.

4

THEY CONVENED IN THE HALLWAY AS INSTRUCTED, AIDEN grumbling about needing to get the camera set up, and Deek moaning about his lack of breakfast. Elspeth stretched, her joints popping. Normally, she was getting out of bed at this time, and now here she was about to make a movie.

The Haunting of Lacey Carmichael.

Elspeth winced just thinking about that title. Their final year at university, and the whole crew's grades hinged on a horror film called *The Haunting of Lacey Carmichael.*

Jeez. She hoped her dissertation, on the use of symbolism in the films of Jean-Luc Godard, would be enough to bolster her grade. Problem was, she wasn't sure she even understood what she was talking about regarding Godard and the French New-Wave. Still, that's what Wikipedia is for, right?

She glanced around at the assembled throng of weary faces. The same crew had worked on Robert's previous two films, so she supposed they all knew what they were getting into. Aiden the cinematographer, Deek the sound-man, and

Laura, of course. She was both producer and assistant director, arguably the two most hated roles on a shoot, and Elspeth thought she was perfect for both.

As Laura sashayed down the hallway alongside Robert, squeezed immaculately into a black-and-white striped dress and heels, Elspeth couldn't help but wonder for the thousandth time how the pair of them had ever become a couple.

Also, who the fuck wears heels to a rainy Scottish film set?

Robert's familiar black leather jacket, which he had worn every day for the last four years, hung loosely over his skeletal frame. He looked like a scrawny film nerd who'd won a competition to go on a date with a supermodel, the two of them the last to arrive at the meeting that Robert himself had called.

They were all in this together, for better or worse, but most likely worse. The only crew member missing today was Gordon Gunn, their editor, a situation born of the deep-seated mutual-loathing between Gordon and Robert. Gordon was no longer welcome on set after the shooting of their first film, during which Gordon had commented that two shots wouldn't cut together and Robert had fought him for "undermining the director in front of the crew". The resulting bout of fisticuffs was the most embarrassing spectacle Elspeth had ever witnessed, and though she liked Gordon a lot, Elspeth thought it was best he stayed away from the pressure cooker of filmmaking.

Two unfamiliar faces stood out. Hannah Morgan and Ted Reilly, their lead actors. Their *only* actors, to be truthful. They looked awfully fresh-faced to be portraying a married couple in the throes of a bitter divorce, but Elspeth guessed that wasn't why Robert had cast the attractive young people.

More likely it was their willingness to strip off for the film's frequent nude scenes.

Oh yes, it wouldn't be a Robert Crawford movie without the all-important nudity.

Elspeth shook her head, resigned to her fate. None of the gang knew, but she had tried to get involved with a different group for her fourth year project. She had even asked to join the documentary crew, who were making a dreary sounding piece about a local baker. By this point, however, the class had devolved into its own distinct cliques, and she found herself lumped back in with Robert and his Z-grade horror movie fantasies.

You made your bed, now lie in it.

Still, maybe this time would be different. Maybe this time they would make something good, or at least watchable. Maybe, maybe, shoulda woulda coulda.

She flashed back to their last film, a regrettable disaster entitled *Burns Night*, in which Scotland's most famous poet Robert Burns had stalked the streets of modern-day Aberdeen as a reanimated zombie, killing prostitutes and dispensing rhyming quips as he did so. The nadir had come at the climax, when the heroic hooker-with-a-heart-of-gold had set the undead writer aflame and turned to the camera, saying, 'It's okay, folks. Tonight, Robert Burns…in Hell.'

Elspeth remembered the laughter from the audience punctuating the scene, then Robert storming out of class, leaving the rest of the crew to shrivel up and die of humiliation.

The Haunting of Lacey Carmichael couldn't possibly be any worse than that, could it? She didn't know. This one was less jokey, more serious. Art with a capital-A, that was how Robert described it. Unfortunately, the only thing more unintentionally funny than a bad comedy horror was a bad *serious* horror. Elspeth had thick skin, but even she didn't want to be a laughing stock for the third year in a row.

'Alright everybody, listen up,' commanded Robert, his face still glowing from the conversation with his uncle. 'Welcome to day one of *The Haunting of Lacey Carmichael*!'

Aiden cheered half-heartedly, everyone else choosing to nod. Most of them had been up since five, fatigue setting in before they had even started shooting.

'This is a film I've had in mind for over a decade. It's a horror film, and a love story, but it's also about so much more than that. It's about the disintegration of the bond between two souls. It's about the fragility of relationships, and—'

Elspeth looked at Deek and Deek looked at Elspeth. She turned away, feeling a fit of the giggles coming on.

'—the impossibility of communication in a technology-driven world. The film takes place simultaneously in the past and the future. We're tackling big ideas here, folks. I can't have any slackers on my team. We've got one day on location. *One day*. You know what that means? It means we can't have any fuck-ups, okay? We've a lot of work to do, a lot of shots, a lot of set-ups.'

I feel so inspired, thought Elspeth. Deek grinned and a smile spread across Elspeth's face. Robert continued.

'I know we've all worked together before, but know this — today, we're not friends. No, today we are *colleagues*, working towards a greater good. There's no time for chit-chat, no time for gossip. We work until we can stand no more, and then we work harder. I want one-hundred and ten percent on this, okay?'

The group nodded again. Not even Aiden bothered to whoop and cheer this time.

'And if you all wanna wake the fuck up,' continued

Robert, 'I'd like to introduce our cast.' He pointed at the two new faces, the only ones still smiling. For an actor, smiling and looking appealing was all part of the job. 'This is Hannah, and this is Ted, our lead actors. Treat them with the respect they deserve, please. Without them, we're nothing.'

Elspeth shot Deek a glance. They both knew Robert didn't believe a word of what he was saying. Only one person mattered on a Robert Crawford movie, and that was the writer-director himself.

'I would also appreciate it if, from now on, you would refer to them using their character names, Lacey and Rex.'

Lacey and Rex. A thin giggle squeaked its way out of Elspeth. It was bad enough that those were the character's names, and now the crew were actually expected to call the actors that to their faces?

'Something funny, Elspeth?' asked Robert. She shook her head, glancing around the assembled group, trying to avoid eye contact with Deek. He winked at her and she almost lost it.

'Okay then,' said Robert. 'Let's make some art.'

Let's make some art.

It was Robert Crawford's favourite phrase, and one he repeated over and over again on every shoot.

Let's make some art.

Elspeth smiled. Robert's definition of art could best be described as *broad*. Still, the old excitement was still there. She could feel the butterflies in her stomach, that sense they were about to embark on a new adventure. Robert often compared filmmaking to war, the troops going into battle with no hope of emerging unscathed from the frontlines. Robert was overdramatic, but the metaphor itself had a grain of truth in it. They all knew nothing ever went to plan, that whatever *could* go wrong, *would* go wrong.

It was part of the thrill.

Elspeth grinned.

Let's make some art.

5

AS FAR AS STUDENT FILM SHOOTS WENT, ELSPETH THOUGHT things were proceeding rather nicely. Okay, so the weather had taken a turn for the worse and all the outdoor scenes had to be hastily rewritten as interiors, and Aiden had left a bag of gels and filters for the lights at home, and Robert's ideas were as banal and unoriginal as they had all feared, but apart from those minor hiccups, the day was going about as well as could be expected. She just hoped it would cut together in the editing room.

Not that it mattered to Elspeth in terms of her grade. She would be marked on production design, costumes and props, rather than the story and filmmaking itself. But still, she wanted to work on a project she could be proud of, one she could show her friends and family. Somehow she doubted *The Haunting of Lacey Carmichael* would be it, but a little hope never hurt anyone.

As she rifled through the black bin-liner that doubled as her prop bag, she heard Robert directing the actors next door.

'Rex, hit her like you mean it, okay?'

'*You want me to really hit her?*'

'*You can't hit me! Robert, he can't hit me!*'

'*No, don't actually hit her, pretend! But make it look real. Let's see the expression, y'know. Hit her with your mind.*'

'*You want me to headbutt her?*'

'*You can't do that! Robert, he can't do that!*'

She imagined Robert's jaw clenching the way it did when he was incandescent with rage. She had seen it many times, even been on the receiving end once or twice. He was one of those guys who was in love with the romanticism of the tortured artist, the put-upon auteur fighting against the relentless grind of The Man. Trouble was, he lacked the talent to back it up. In a way, she felt sorry for him, then reneged on the idea. Robert was rich — hell, his uncle owned this mansion — and would never have to worry about anything as long as his dad's credit card was tucked snugly in his pocket.

She emptied the contents of the bag onto the bed and set some items aside. A towel, a hairbrush, a silk robe, all in preparation for the next scene, the one Robert and the boys were undoubtedly looking forward to the most.

The shower scene.

It wasn't the first time they had filmed nudity — *Burns Night* had its fair share of topless wenches being menaced by Scotland's undead bard — but it was unusual in that Robert always ensured the nude scenes were filmed first; that way, if an actress refused, he hadn't wasted any time filming her and could quickly hire someone new. He was nothing if not mercenary. Elspeth wondered why Robert had left the nudity until last. Perhaps because he knew he couldn't get a replacement even if he wanted to? Did the risk of being left out here without an actress outweigh the risk of not getting one of his precious boob shots?

She checked her phone. It was already after six, so she decided to go and see what was happening. Downstairs, a door slammed. Robert's uncle? She hadn't even been introduced to him, but supposed he was simply keeping out of their way. It was for the best. Nothing derails a shoot quite like a curious onlooker.

Voices leaked through the door, and Elspeth assumed they were between takes. Out of habit, she put her ear to the door to check, then entered. It was another bedroom, this one decked out entirely in different shades of purple. The curtains, the carpet, the bedspread — she half expected to see Prince strumming a guitar in the corner. She sidled up to Laura, engrossed, as usual, in her script notes.

'How much longer?'

'Hmm? Oh, not long. They'll be ready in ten minutes or so,' replied Laura without looking up. Elspeth smiled at Deek, his little round head dwarfed by enormous studio-headphones. He raised his eyebrows at her. Hannah and Ted chatted animatedly to each other, both talking about themselves, neither listening to the other, like two old folks in a dementia ward.

'Where's Robert?'

Laura didn't even deign to acknowledge her this time, so Aiden stepped in.

'Gone to get something from the car.'

'Like what?'

Aiden shrugged and turned the camera on her.

'I don't know, Elspeth. What do *you* think it is?'

She glared at him. 'What are you doing?'

'Behind the scenes. DVD extras.'

'No one buys DVDs anymore,' said Deek too loudly, the headphones obscuring his hearing. 'Not even my dad.'

'The kid's got a point,' said Elspeth, adopting the tone of

a jaded, cigar-smoking studio executive. 'Maybe we should just livestream the whole movie to Facebook.'

'No one uses *Facebook* anymore, Elspeth,' laughed Deek. He shook his head. 'Not even my *dad*.'

Elspeth bit her tongue to stop her telling Deek that if he searched hard enough, her *MySpace* page could still be found online. Actually, he probably wouldn't even know what she was talking about.

'The thing with physical media is—' began Aiden, before being mercifully cut short by Robert flouncing triumphantly into the room. Elspeth wasn't in the mood for one of Aiden's patronising lectures on cinema and the death of physical media, or the pros and cons of digital film-making versus analogue. He was the sort of person she always ended up sitting next to at parties, spending the evening listening to him pontificate at length about the history of industrial music or whether time itself is purely a construct, while she tried to think up excuses to leave and join the people who were drinking and having fun.

Her glee at Robert's entrance was short-lived when she saw he was carrying a shotgun.

'Jesus,' she said, thoughts of Robert blowing them all away flashing through her mind.

'Aw shite, is that real?' asked Deek, his face a mask of wonderment.

'Sure is,' said Robert.

'Can I hold it?'

Laura stormed to her feet and wrenched the weapon from Robert. 'What the fuck are you doing bringing a gun to set?'

'It's not loaded,' said Robert defensively.

'I don't give a shit!' Laura was flying now, and the rest of the crew made themselves comfortable. Where's the popcorn when you really need it?

'You didn't tell me! It's not on the Risk Assessment!' Robert tried to speak, to make excuses, but Laura talked over him. 'Where did you get a gun from? Was that in your car? Did we drive all the way here with a gun in the car?'

'I—'

'Do you even have a licence? What if the police had stopped us?'

'It's my dad's. I thought it'd be good for the scene. Lacey threatens Rex with the shotgun, forces him out of the house, y'know?'

'I could have got you a fake shotgun,' said Elspeth, even more annoyed to discover Robert had taken part of her job. 'It's what I'm supposed to be doing on this shoot.'

He shot her a look. 'I was *trying* to do you a favour.'

'Then do me a favour and put that gun back where you found it.'

'I don't want to shoot a gun,' said Hannah, her voice infuriatingly timid. Robert turned his attention to her, the youngest person on set.

The easiest target.

'You wouldn't be shooting it. You'd be acting! You know, the thing you're being paid to do.'

'Wait, is she being paid?' said Ted. He looked at Hannah. 'Is he paying you?'

Hannah looked at Laura. 'Am I being paid?'

'No one's being paid!' shouted Robert. 'You know what? Fucking forget it!' He snatched the gun back from Laura and stormed out of the room. The tension was palpable and Elspeth could take no more. She cleared her throat.

'So Aiden, what were you saying about physical media?'

When Robert returned, his expression as stormy as a Scottish winter, Elspeth excused herself to the actors' room until they finished. The only thing worse than Robert the Director was moody Robert the Director sulking his way through a scene with a face like a smacked arse.

Twenty minutes later, and with the clock rapidly ticking towards finishing time, the door swung open and Hannah appeared, throwing herself down onto the bed atop the props that Elspeth had carefully laid out. Ted followed, dragging an antique chair from out of the corner. Elspeth raised her hand to stop him.

'I don't think we're supposed to sit—'

He plonked himself down on the chair, which groaned beneath his muscular frame. It probably hadn't been sat in for a hundred years. Elspeth turned away, shaking her head.

'I'm knackered,' sighed Hannah from the bed.

'You guys finished the scene?' asked Elspeth. 'Did it go okay?'

Ted cracked open a Coke, the can fizzing and spilling foam on the carpet. He either didn't notice or didn't care. Elspeth guessed the latter.

'Hey, careful,' she said, rushing over and dabbing at the shaggy carpet with a cloth.

'It went great,' he said. 'Eh, Hannah?'

'Yeah. I just wish he'd stop shouting.'

'Who, Robert?' Elspeth looked around, trying to see what else Ted could spill.

'Yeah. We've to get dressed for the next scene,' said Hannah. 'Well, just me. Ted's not in this one.'

'Do I get to watch?' he asked, grinning at Hannah.

'No chance, you perv,' smiled Hannah, but Elspeth thought she could see the nerves behind her eyes.

'Alright Ted, give us some privacy, will you? I'll help Hannah get ready.'

Ted shrugged and got up. 'No problem,' he said, leaving the two girls alone in the room.

Elspeth sat next to Hannah. 'You okay?'

Hannah studied her like a zoo exhibit. 'Yeah. Why?'

'Just, y'know, the next scene...' She waited for Hannah to catch on. She didn't. 'I thought you might be nervous.'

'Oh, the shower scene? No, it's okay.' She looked Elspeth up and down. 'I'm confident about my body.' Elspeth tried not to read anything into the comment.

'Okay. Good.' *You should be*, she almost added, then scolded herself. This was no time for flirting. Instead, she handed Hannah a pale blue blouse and a pair of Levi's. 'Here, put these on.'

'Thanks, Elizabeth,'

'It's Elspeth.'

Hannah smiled sweetly at her. 'That's what I said.'

6

THE CREW WATCHED IN SILENCE AS HANNAH UNDRESSED, THE rain drumming softly against the bathroom window like so many bony fingers. Slowly, methodically, playing up every action for maximum effect, she worked the buttons of the light-blue cotton blouse free.

Robert stroked his hand through his beard. She was good. Very good. He almost felt bad about not paying her.

Hannah shrugged off her blouse and it drifted to the tiled floor like an autumn leaf. Then she turned her back on them, reaching round and unclasping her bra.

Nice touch, thought Robert. *Show the sizzle before the steak.*

She held the bra out and it too ended up on the floor, where she nudged it to one side with her toes.

Robert suppressed a nervous giggle. She turned and he nodded, his thin lips curving into a smile.

She glanced past him, cocking her head.

'Hello? Is anyone there?'

Her voice was flat. Deadpan.

'Rex? Is that you?'

He licked his lips. *Okay, okay, good, nailed it. Now the jeans. Take them off.*

She shrugged exaggeratedly. 'Must be my igamination. Shit, I mean imagination.'

Jesus Christ.

'Keep going,' urged Robert, conscious of Father Time breathing lustily down his neck.

He glanced at the monitor, the frame filled with an image of the topless girl. The lighting was beautiful, but the framing was off-centre. Fucking Aiden, too distracted by her tits. Still, if the audience was looking at the composition of the scene rather than Hannah's breasts, there was something very wrong with them. Christ, he knew she was a terrible actress, but finding someone willing to act in a student film *and* get fully nude was harder than he had expected, particularly for no money.

She unhooked her belt and fiddled with the brass button on her jeans. Robert realised he had been holding his breath. He exhaled.

Get to the goods, dammit. You're going too slow.

But she couldn't get it undone. She pulled and pulled on the jeans, the button stuck. Robert checked the monitor. Her face wasn't in the shot, Aiden having zoomed in to below her neckline. The money shot.

'Fuck,' she said, shaking her head in irritation as she wrestled with the errant fastener.

'Need any help?' sneered Robert. Behind the camera, Aiden chuckled.

'Can we start again?'

Robert looked at Laura. She checked her watch.

'No time.'

'You heard her,' said Robert. 'Keep going. And make it sexier. And faster.'

He knew Laura was giving him the stink-eye. She was opposed to the whole scene, thought it was crass and exploitative. Well, *duh*. They weren't making *Lawrence of Arabia* here. Tits and arse were expected in a horror flick. Demanded, even. He figured Laura knew that too. She understood the harsh realities of independent film-making as well as anyone. She just didn't like him filming it. It made her jealous, and that in turn made Robert happy. It proved she still wanted him.

Hannah shivered and went back to her jeans, managing to successfully pop the button. It was cold, and he could see the gooseflesh on her arms in the HD monitor. She slid the jeans over her hips, trying to make it look seductive, then stumbled as she stepped out of them. Robert grimaced.

She can't even get undressed convincingly.

But boy, did she look good. She hooked her thumbs in the waistband of her underpants and hesitated.

What now?

'Take them off,' said Robert.

'Do I have to?'

'*Yes.*'

Hannah tugged them down slightly and stopped again. Robert felt his blood-pressure rising.

'It's just that...I'd rather not, if that's okay.'

'Jesus Christ, *cut*.' His body was tense and he tried not to show his frustration.

Aiden hit the button and finished the recording, the room visibly relaxing. Robert glared at Hannah. She looked so vulnerable and frightened. It was the best piece of acting he had seen from her, and the camera wasn't even rolling.

'What's the problem? You told me you were okay with nudity.'

She shrugged again. 'Yeah, but I thought you meant my boobs. Can't I keep my underwear on?'

'You ever shower with your knickers on?'

'No,' she said in a small voice. 'But, I mean, what's the point of this scene? Is it an excuse to see me naked?'

Robert was prepared for this line of questioning. He had already gone over it with Laura, and knew it would come up again with his university tutors at the final screening.

'Of course not,' he lied. 'We're playing with archetypes here, deconstructing them. There's a certain ubiquity to classic horror film tropes that must be met in order to comment on the facile limitations of the genre.'

He knew none of that made any sense, but hoped no one would question it. Hannah regarded him blankly.

'Oh,' was all she said.

'Oh indeed.'

'We're running out of time,' said Laura. 'We better get a move on.'

'Let's just get the shot,' snapped Robert. He fixed Hannah with a death-stare. 'Unless our little ingenue has any more questions?'

Her face reddened in embarrassment.

'No.'

'Good. Aiden, you ready?'

'Sure thing mate.'

'Hannah?'

'You promise there's no...close-ups?'

Robert relished the way she squirmed as she asked the question.

'I promise.'

I'm such a good liar, maybe I should have been an actor instead of a director.

'Okay, are we ready?' asked Robert. 'Let's get this in one

take. Remember, you're not just showering, you're scrubbing your body free of the past, of your haunted memories. Rex used to fixate on your breasts, so I want you to focus on them. Grab that soap and give them a real good scrub, okay?'

'Because that makes sense,' said Elspeth from somewhere behind him, his own personal heckler.

'Will the water be hot?' asked Hannah.

'Can't do that, I'm afraid,' answered Aiden. 'Lens would steam up.'

Robert signalled to Elspeth. 'Clapper ready?'

Elspeth nodded, holding the old-fashioned slate board in front of the lens.

'Sound rolling,' said Deek.

'Camera rolling,' said Aiden.

Elspeth held the slate. 'Scene six, shot one, take two.' She slammed the clapstick shut. Robert took a deep breathe.

'And...action!'

Hannah resumed her performance, slipping out of her underwear. Robert smiled, then noticed Laura was staring at him. He turned back to Hannah.

God, he wanted to fuck her.

He wouldn't, of course. He may be an asshole, but he was loyal to Laura, maybe even loved her. But that didn't stop him wanting to fuck Hannah. And you know what? There were plenty of people willing to pay to imagine doing just that. How many other student films would have explicit nudity? None, he wagered. Every film needs a selling point.

Hannah turned away, her bare arse filling the monitor as Aiden zoomed in again. Robert silently cursed. He hated that seventies aesthetic, the zoom lens flying in and out like the camera was attached to a trombone.

Hannah stepped over the side of the bath, then pressed

the switch. The shower head rattled and burst into life, hitting her with a jet of water between her breasts.

'Oh fuck it's freezing,' she shouted, staggering backwards, her feet slipping out from under her. She groped blindly for something, *anything*, grabbing a handful of shower curtain. It did nothing to arrest her fall.

The room uniformly winced in anticipation as Hannah fell, ripping the curtain from the rail and taking it with her. She collapsed hard on her back, crying out in pain. Elspeth dropped the clapper-board and rushed to help her, her own leg accidentally kicking the tripod. It started to fall and Robert instinctively leapt forward, catching it a fraction of a second before all two-thousand pounds of camera equipment shattered on the hardwood floor.

'Fuck, what was that?' he shouted, his heart racing.

Elspeth helped Hannah out of the bath and wrapped a towel around her.

'I'm sorry,' Hannah said through tears. 'The water was so cold.'

Robert pounded his fist off the wall. 'Jesus, you're meant to be an actress. *Pretend* it's hot!'

'Ignore him,' said Elspeth, putting an arm around her. Then, to Robert, she said, 'Who gets in the shower and then turns on the water? It's not realistic.'

Robert lifted the camera and held it while Aiden adjusted the legs of the tripod. 'Realistic? Who cares about realism? We're making a horror film, Elspeth. Normal cinematic rules don't apply. I don't deal in reality, I deal in dreams and nightmares, fantasy and illusion.'

'Aye, you're living in a fantasy all right,' muttered Elspeth loud enough for him to hear.

'Listen little girl, you just stick to set design and leave the direction to the real artists, okay?'

The bathroom door swung open and struck the tripod. This time Aiden was ready and caught the camera, fumbled it, and then held it firm. Another disaster narrowly averted.

Welcome to the world of student filmmaking.

'What now?' shrieked Robert. 'Are we making a fucking Marx Brothers movie all of a sudden?' He was losing control of his set. It was a director's worst nightmare.

The old man in the doorway surveyed the scene. The torn shower curtain, the water-soaked tiles, the crying girl. His bathroom, in a state of incredible disrepair. Laura noticed him first.

'Oh shit, Mr Crawford, I'm sorry about the mess. We'll tidy it up, I promise.'

He cut her off. His cold eyes seemed to look through her and she felt like there was a ghost lurking over her shoulder.

'It's seven-thirty.' He said. 'You need to be gone in half an hour.'

With that, he turned and walked away.

'Okay,' said Laura quietly. 'Great talking to you.'

Robert clenched his fists. Hannah's insufferable sniffling was getting on his already frayed nerves.

'Fine. I can't take any more of this amateur-hour bollocks. Five-minute break to reset for the final take. Aiden, can we review the footage please?'

7

TED WAS SITTING IN THE CHAIR TAKING SELFIES WHEN Hannah, clad only in a towel, burst in, closely followed by Elspeth.

'Out,' demanded Elspeth.

'What? This is the actors' room, and I'm the lead actor.'

'I'm the lead,' sniffed Hannah. 'My name's in the title.'

'I get more dialogue.'

Elspeth gave him a withering stare. 'Could you just leave please?'

'Why do I always have to go? What happened in there?'

'Just get out, or I'll fucking throw you out, understand?' she snapped. Annoyed, Ted stormed off, and Elspeth perched next to Hannah on the four-poster bed, the opulent lace curtains spider-webbing over her shoulders. She had only ever seen a bedroom like this in the movies, and here she was in a house that had about ten of them. Like the rest, the bed did not appear to have ever been slept in.

It was torn from the pages of a fairy tale, a room fit for a princess, from the crystal chandelier to the teak wardrobe and dressing table. The carpet was so luxurious that it was like walking through grass. It made her job as set designer easy. Too easy, in fact. Would her tutors mark her unfairly if they knew how little work she had actually done, how all the bizarre knick-knacks were already on location when they arrived?

Oil paintings of old, dead white guys? Check.

Ostentatious furniture? Check.

Cushions with dogs in hunting gear stitched onto them? Somehow, check.

It was ridiculous, the faded grandeur seeping from every pore in the redbrick walls. Medieval tapestries, Ming vases, everything except a taxidermy bear at the end of the ground-floor hallway.

No, wait, that was there too, beneath a mounted deer skull, *naturally*. There was quite the menagerie of stuffed animals, layers of grime caking their moth-eaten coats.

It left Elspeth with little to do. The costumes she had supplied were nothing to write home about. If only Robert had made it a period piece! Instead, he had asked for jeans and t-shirts. Only Hannah's diaphanous gown stood out as anything interesting, and that was mainly notable for how see-through it was.

The problem, as usual, was that Robert was more inter-ested in blood and boobs than anything else, and she constantly found herself fighting against him to do her job. Hell, *her* grades were reliant on the success of this stupid, crummy little movie too. The shotgun should have been the final straw, but it was too late to stop now.

Hannah sniffed back tears and Elspeth took the girl's hand.

'How's your back? Want me to take a look?'

Hannah nodded glumly. 'It hurts.'

'Okay. Wait a sec.' Elspeth sauntered to the door and slid

the lock into place. Poor Hannah had been ogled enough today. When she turned, Hannah was naked, the towel at her feet. She faced away from Elspeth, a deep yellow and purple mark on her lower back marring her otherwise flawless skin.

There goes the continuity again.

'Shit, Hannah, it's gonna bruise.'

'Really? How bad?'

Elspeth inspected the damage, lightly pressing a finger to the base of Hannah's spine. The girl squealed.

'Pretty bad.'

'Will Robert be angry?'

'Don't worry about him, he's all talk.'

Hannah turned to face her, black mascara tears running down her cheeks.

'Do you think he'll fire me?'

Elspeth smiled. 'Nah, he couldn't even if he wanted to. He doesn't have time to replace you. This is our only day here, remember?'

Plus, no one else is crazy enough to star in this piece of shit movie, let alone get their tits out for it.

'But he could shoot somewhere else. With a different actress, I mean.'

'Impossible. Who's gonna fill in at this short notice? Me?'

Hannah's face brightened. 'You're right. You wouldn't be able to. Acting is hard.' She smiled and squeezed Elspeth's hand.

'Thanks, Elizabeth,' she said.

'It's Elspeth.'

'Oh yeah. That's a funny name.'

Hannah dressed while Elspeth politely looked away, stealing the occasional glance at her in the mirror. She felt sorry for Hannah, who was seemingly unaware she was being ruthlessly exploited by an unscrupulous director. Robert was a hack, and the only reason he had achieved a passing grade so far was thanks to his editor, Gordon Gunn.

She wished Gordon was here. He possessed all the talent that Robert believed he had, with none of the confidence. It was a shame. She had sat in the editing suite during their first film together and watched him shape the formless mass of Robert's footage into something resembling a real movie. If not for Gordon's skills, *The Grave That Yawned* would have been laughed off the screen. Instead, it just bored people to tears. Sandy had said *The Audience That Yawned* would be a more appropriate title, and Elspeth couldn't argue. Damn, she wished Sandy was here too.

Well, maybe not right this second, she thought, catching Hannah's nude reflection in the mirror again.

She remembered how Robert had been incandescent with rage when he watched the final cut of his film. Gordon had pared back the director's worst excesses, cutting expertly around the appalling performances and shaky hand-held camera work, shuffling the scenes into a less linear and more interesting order. If he only believed in himself, and was willing to speak up, he could really go places. Why were the most talented people always the quietest, while the bolshy loud-mouths manage to bully their way to success through sheer force of will?

Poor Hannah. She had neither the talent nor the willpower, though sometimes beauty was enough. She sat down next to Elspeth, pulling on her socks.

'You know,' said Elspeth, 'You don't have to take Robert's shit.'

'But he's the director.'

'He couldn't direct traffic.' She put her hand on Hannah's

shoulder and considered how to best to say it. 'He's using you, y'know.'

'He said he liked my demo reel.'

I'll bet he did.

'Well, if you ever feel uncomfortable, don't be afraid to say anything. Or let me know, and I'll say something for you. We're all in this together, you know.'

Hannah laughed. 'But you're not an actress.'

'No, I mean *women*. We have to stick together. We can't let men use us.'

Hannah buttoned up her blouse and shook her head as if Elspeth was being silly. 'Well, thank you Elizabeth, but I'm fine. Anyway, Robert said you wouldn't see anything. No close-ups. It's art. Like those old paintings you see. That's why he says that thing. Let's make some art.'

Elspeth nodded.

Sure. And if you believe that, you're even dumber than you look.

8

IT DIDN'T TAKE LONG FOR HANNAH TO REALISE ELSPETH WAS telling the truth.

Fifteen seconds to be precise, the time it took her to walk from the actors' room to the bathroom.

'What the fuck!' she screamed, her voice echoing through the corridors of Crawford Manor.

Robert was crouched next to Aiden, the two of them staring intently at the monitor. He saw the shocked look on the face of his lead actress and immediately switched into damage limitation mode.

'It's not what you think,' he said, getting up and positioning his feet in front of the screen, wagging his finger at her like a school-teacher.

'Not what I think? That's my fucking vagina!'

'No,' he stuttered, 'Well, yes, it is, but we weren't going to use that shot.'

'Move your foot,' said Elspeth, squeezing her way into the already crowded room.

'Look, we just—'

'Move it!'

Sheepishly, Robert did so, revealing a close-up of Hannah's bare crotch in glorious 1080p high-definition.

'Oh my god,' gasped Hannah. 'Play the whole scene.'

'Listen,' said Robert, coming towards her. She shoved him back.

'No, I don't want to hear it. Just play the scene, from start to finish.'

'We can reshoot.'

'Play the scene!'

Cornered, he nodded at Aiden, who took the Canon 7D camera and skipped back to the start of the shot. Hannah, Elspeth and Laura crowded round and watched it unfold, Hannah's face visibly darkening with fury at each zoom. The first was into her breasts. Then, it pulled back, cutting her head off at the neck.

'You can't even see my *face*.'

There was a bit of faffing as she fiddled with the button on her jeans, then the whole conversation, and a zoom that finished on an extreme close-up.

'You bastard,' said Elspeth. Robert glared at her with thinly veiled fury.

'You keep out of this. Listen, Hannah, I'm sorry. We can—'

'Forget it,' she yelled. 'I'm done here.'

Robert searched around for assistance from his crew. He glanced at Laura, but she was giving him daggers. Elspeth would be no help. Aiden stared at the wall like a right wimp, and Deek, headphones covering his ears, apparently hadn't noticed there was an argument taking place. It was all on Robert now, and for once he was speechless.

'I quit,' said Hannah.

'You can't. We've already shot a day's worth of film! If you quit now, we're up shit creek. We're fucked!' He tried not to raise his voice, but he was fighting a losing battle with himself.

Hannah smiled. He could have punched her there and then.

'Good,' she said. 'Maybe you'll learn something. Elizabeth was right, you know. I don't have to take your shit.'

With that, she stormed out of the bathroom. Robert took several deep breaths and fixed his eyes on Elspeth.

Elspeth made a face. 'Wow, that Elizabeth sounds like a real bitch, huh?'

She waited for Robert to lose it, to launch into one of his familiar tirades.

But why should she be nervous? It was his fault. Him and Aiden. She hadn't been the one to lie to an actress.

Robert's shark-eyes bored holes into her skin. His fists were clenched. She had seen him angry before, but never like this. He spoke slowly, enunciating every syllable like he was chewing them up.

'I don't know what you fucking said, or what you fucking did, but you had better go fix it right this fucking minute, or else we are all well and truly *fucked*.'

'It's not my problem.'

'You're right,' said Aiden. 'It's *our* problem now, thanks to you.'

Elspeth looked to Laura for back-up. Girl power, right?

'What the fuck are we going to do without a lead actress? Go and get her.'

Elspeth shook her head in dismay. She couldn't believe no one had her back. Even Deek just sat staring at his hands and biting his lower lip. 'Okay, sure. How about I rewind time to stop those perverts zooming in on a nineteen-year-old's fanny?'

No one said anything. She felt like an actress in her own

film, one where her friends all turned out to be sleazy, spineless cowards. She hoped it would have a happy ending.

'Fine, I'll go,' she said, leaving the bad atmosphere of the bathroom behind. She walked down the hall to the actor's room, the sixth door on the left. The sixth! And to think Mr Crawford lived here alone. What on Earth did he need with a ten-bedroom house?

You're getting distracted.

A hand on her shoulder startled her.

'Sorry,' said Deek. 'Didnae mean to frighten you.'

'It's fine,' said Elspeth, though her racing heart told a different story. 'Thanks for the help in there, by the way.'

Deek coloured. 'Ah, I'm sorry. You know what Robert's like.'

'Aye, I do. Just would've been nice if you'd said something.'

He changed the subject. 'You gonna talk to her?'

'I'm trying to.'

'Want me to come with you?'

Elspeth almost laughed. 'Aye, Deek, I'm sure that's exactly what the angry actress wants to see right now. Your big gormless face.' She saw Deek's expression change, and sighed. 'Shit, I didn't mean that. Just go back, okay? I'll have a talk with her. You try and calm Robert down or something.'

She knocked and let herself in, leaving Deek prowling outside.

'Hey,' said Elspeth softly.

Hannah angrily pulled on her t-shirt, a glittery pug emblazoned on the front, pink tongue drooping from his grinning mouth. 'I can't believe that bastard. He lied to me!'

Elspeth threw herself on the bed and tucked her hands behind her head.

'I know.'

'So what, are you here to talk me out of it? Has he sent you to change my mind? Or are you here to say *I told you so*?'

Elspeth watched Hannah through the fine lace curtains of the four-poster bed. She was gauzy, indistinct.

'He did send me, yes. To sweet talk you. But I'm not going to.'

Hannah pulled on her jeans and looked at Elspeth, cocking her head in an unconscious imitation of the pug on her shirt.

'Really? But won't that mess up your film?'

Elspeth nodded. 'Yeah. But don't worry about it. It's shit anyway. We can save it in the edit, turn it into a psychedelic art film or something.'

Hannah lay down next to Elspeth and looked at her curiously. 'I don't mind staying, you know. As long as he deletes the footage.'

'I know. Which is why I'm telling you to leave. You don't owe us anything. Fuck Robert and his stupid movie. He has no right to treat people that way.'

Hannah stared for an uncomfortably long time, a single tear rolling down her pink cheek.

'Thank you, Elizabeth.'

This time Elspeth didn't bother correcting her. Hannah left the bed and grabbed her bag. 'Guess I'll be heading off.'

'How will you get home? Didn't Aiden drive you?'

'I'll phone for a taxi.'

'Back to Aberdeen? That'll cost a fortune. Why not wait in my car and I'll drive you in about fifteen minutes?'

Hannah shook her head. 'I can't. I can't see Robert again, can't even look at him. At *any* of them.'

She hugged Elspeth and went to the door.

'It was nice to meet you.'

'You too, Hannah. And don't let anyone take advantage of you again, okay?'

Hannah raised a hand and waved. 'I won't. Say goodbye to Ted for me.'

The door closed gently behind her and then Elspeth was alone on the king-size bed, the howling gale outside battering the window panes.

She sat for a moment, catching her reflection in the mirror.

'What the fuck have I done,' she said to herself.

Her reflection stared back at her, saying nothing.

Hannah crept along the hallway, the old wooden floor-boards creaking with every step. Thankfully, the bathroom was beyond the staircase and she wouldn't have to walk past them all.

Particularly Robert. That creep!

Her anger was fading, replaced by a disgusted feeling of degradation. How could someone do this to her? He promised the nudity would not be, what was that word he used...*gratuitous*, that was it. It wouldn't be *gratuitous*. Well he had a pretty funny idea of what *that* word meant, presuming it meant what she thought it did. The idea that the footage was on the camera appalled her. He might never delete it. He could even still use it in the film!

She would sue him. Yeah, she'd hire a lawyer like in those American films, and *sue his ass*. Failing that, she would get her cousin Adam to smash his face in. That was the more likely scenario, if she was being honest. Well, once he got out of jail, anyway.

The other thing she felt was pride. Pride in the fact that

she had stood up for herself, for quitting and walking away from a lead role in a film, even if it was a silly student one. That would show them! She only hoped they wouldn't tell anyone. Word had a way of getting round about 'difficult' actresses.

Difficult.

Yeah, like they were the problem. You're only seen as difficult if you won't suck the director's dick, or agree to a closeup of your vagina being splashed across a cinema screen. And if you refuse, you're labelled — no, *branded* — as being difficult.

She reached the bottom of the stairs, her Converse scuffing over the floor as leering animal heads watched her with marble eyes. She arrived at the front door and tried the handle.

It was locked.

'Shit,' she said through gritted teeth. She ran both hands through her hair and turned back, facing down the hallway. She had to find the owner. What was his name again? Ah yes, Crawford.

Mr Crawford of Crawford Manor, at your service.

He would let her out, and hopefully call a taxi. Damn, was he her only option? She had met Mr Crawford briefly at the start of the day, and found him frightening. He was too tall, too old. He had looked Hannah up and down, appraising her like a slab of meat in a butcher shop. She wanted desperately for someone else to talk to him, but she couldn't go back up the stairs, not now, not ever again.

Instead, Hannah made her way along the corridor, trying not to look at the huge stuffed bear at the far end. It was posed as if about to attack, its arms raised, claws bared, mouth in a devilish snarl.

It had probably been shot in the back while sleeping.

She looked down both corridors, realising she had no idea where Mr Crawford could be. She listened, hearing the faint sounds of the crew arguing upstairs. No sign of the old man, though she knew he had to be downstairs. She chose left. There were six doors down the corridor. She tried the first one, knocking before entering, as her mother had taught her to do.

It was a living room, garishly decorated in golds and reds. A huge marble fireplace sat cold and distant, the gilt-edged mirror above it split by a hairline crack.

But no Mr Crawford.

She backed out and tried the next door. Locked. She knocked, afraid to call out, but no one answered. She went to the last door on the left and tapped her knuckles against the old oak, twisting the handle. It was also locked.

Hannah was on the verge of tears. All she wanted was to get a taxi and go home, was that too much to ask? She turned her back on the door, and then she heard it.

Click.

The door behind her unlocked.

Hannah shivered. 'Hello?' she called out, hoping the crew upstairs wouldn't hear her. There was no response. She turned the handle again and this time the door gave way. A musty smell, old but not unpleasant, seeped from inside. The dying embers of daylight forced their way through the ragged curtains, casting a crimson tint, illuminating an archaic wooden crib in the centre of the room.

That wasn't the problem though. It was the walls.

They were lined with shelves, from floor to ceiling, and on those shelves were perched hundreds and hundreds of dolls.

'You're kidding me on,' whispered Hannah.

The shelves stretched across all four walls, only stopping

for the doorway and the solitary window. The dolls themselves were mostly hideous, their cracked ceramic faces weathering years of abandonment. Some were missing eyes, others went without clothes, their bodies carved from what looked like lumps of misshapen timber. There were baby dolls and pirate dolls, sailor dolls and clowns.

Too many clowns.

In the corner were bigger dolls, life-size, stacked atop one another like a funeral pyre.

The one thing that united them was that they all seemed to be staring at Hannah through their ugly, shattered faces. Why was everything in this house always watching?

She turned her attention to the crib, noticing for the first time that it was rocking.

A fly buzzed past Hannah's face and she swatted it away. Against her better judgement, she found herself walking towards the crib. Was there something in it? The door closed behind her and she jumped, then laughed, pretending she was being silly.

There's nothing to be scared of, she told herself.

She reached the crib and placed a hand on it. There, tucked under the covers, was a little mound. She glanced around. There were no other doors in here, none that she could see at least. Who let her in? And where were they now?

She didn't notice the trapdoor above her.

She scanned the rows, anything to prolong pulling back the sheet. The way the light fell across the dolls made the ceramic look like bone, hundreds of grinning children's skulls just sitting there, indifferent to their fate. Her head turned sharply towards the pile in the corner. Had one of them moved?

No, of course not.

She held the tiny bed sheet with trembling hands and pulled it away like a magician revealing a trick.

Hannah almost screamed.

It's a baby, it's a dead baby.

But it wasn't, and she didn't. It was just another doll, blue and lifeless, the porcelain chipped and spider-webbed. Its eyes were black pits and she looked away, afraid that she would somehow fall in and never be seen again.

A door opened out in the hallway, wrenching Hannah from her imagination. She fled the room, leaving the crib rocking behind her, heart beating too fast, bursting out into the hallway in time to hear the same door slamming shut.

'Oh thank god,' she sighed, marching down the corridor. 'Mr Crawford? Excuse me, Mr Crawford? I need the keys. I need to go home.'

There was no acknowledgement, no sound.

She quickened her pace, jogging now, heading for the door, forgetting her manners and not knocking, just pushing it open and barging in. An office. Nothing unexpected there, apart from the distinct lack of Mr Crawford.

Where *was* he?

There was another door in the corner, a large metal one, the kind you find in a hotel kitchen or something. A meat locker. It was utterly incongruous among the ancient relics of Crawford Manor. She could hear sounds coming from beyond, the sounds of working, of manual labour.

'Mr Crawford?'

The noises stopped. Hannah reached the door and pushed it open.

'Oh god,' she said, her eyes darting across the room. 'Oh Jesus Christ.'

Only then did the smell hit her, a charnel house stench that flipped her stomach as she struggled to take in the obscenity before her, her mind performing mental backflips to comprehend the bizarre horror behind the door.

'Please,' she said, 'I won't tell. I won't tell *anyone*. Just please, let me go.'

She staggered backwards and he came for her.

She had one chance to make it to the hallway. There, she could scream, alert the others. They would come to her rescue, save her. She turned on her heels and ran, bumping into the door, reaching for the handle.

She thought she could make it. She was fast.

She wasn't fast enough.

9

'SO WHAT THE HELL ARE WE GONNA DO?'

It was Deek who vocalised what they were all thinking. Laura checked her watch. It had become automatic for her. As Producer and Assistant Director, it was her job to make sure that everything went to schedule. She ran the sets with an iron fist, even Robert acquiescing to her demands. But now Laura, the great problem solver, was stumped.

'I guess we're fucked,' was all she could think to say.

Robert sat slumped against the bathroom wall, his head in his hands. 'And you *tried* to talk her out of it?'

Elspeth thought it best to fudge the truth. No point in starting an argument. 'Yeah, her mind was made up. You pushed her too far.'

'Bullshit,' he said, his voice muffled behind his palms, the halogen spotlights making him look pale and drawn. Light rain spattered off the window.

'Maybe if you'd paid her?'

'And where are we going to conjure up the money for that?' said Laura icily. 'Last I heard, none of us were exactly rolling in cash.'

Elspeth considered mentioning Robert's wealthy parents, then thought better of it.

'How much is left? Can Gordon salvage it in the edit?'

'Impossible,' said Robert. 'We still have half the film to shoot. Big scenes, important scenes.'

'You mean like the sex scene?' interjected Elspeth. Neither Robert nor Laura looked amused.

'That's a very important scene, actually. It shows the developing bond between Lacey and Rex.'

Elspeth ground her teeth together. *Lacey and Rex.*

Her grades hinged entirely on a horror film about Lacey and fucking *Rex*.

'We can still shoot all the scenes with Ted,' said Aiden, trying to be helpful.

'That's fine with me,' said Ted, surprising everyone. Most of them had forgotten he was even there.

Robert leaned back theatrically, his head thudding off the wall. 'And what? They only share a couple of scenes? He's meant to be *haunting* her for fuck's sake!'

Aiden threw his hands up in submission. He knew better than to debate with Robert.

'It's almost eight,' said Laura. 'We're out of time.'

Robert stood up. 'Go to the cars. And leave everything behind.'

'Rob, we have to get the equipment outta here. That'll take at least twenty minutes. Your uncle will be raging.'

'No, I'm gonna talk to him. Straighten a few things out. I'll get us another day tomorrow, okay?'

'But we don't have an actress,' said Elspeth.

Robert glared at her. 'Just shut up, okay? You got us into this. I'm trying to dig us out. All of you, just go out and wait outside. Can you do that much for me?'

With a collective shrug, the group dispersed, a black mood descending.

Only Robert remained. He stayed in the bathroom a little longer.

Thinking. Figuring things out.

At seven-fifty-five, he jogged down the stairs and hesitated in front of his uncle's door. He knocked, listening to the bolts slipping out of place, the key in the lock, and the creak of the door as it yawned open.

'Yes?'

Robert cleared his throat. 'I was wondering—'

'No. You need to be out in five minutes. I presume you have removed any and all of your equipment from the premises? Anything left behind I will consider my own personal property, and dispose of accordingly.'

Robert nodded. 'Absolutely. I just wanted to say thanks.' The sarcasm was duly noted. Crawford stared at him with piercing eyes.

'I don't ever want to hear from you again, son. And that goes for your father too.'

'No problem,' smiled Robert. He waited until the door slammed in his face and carried on down the hall.

Crawford — he would have been Ross to his friends, but he had none — slipped back into his office and sat, hands clasped neatly on the desk, the relentless *tick-tock* of the clock his only company. Occasionally he heard the girl next door, the soft thump of her head against the wall.

She was nearly finished.

They never lasted.

He supposed they didn't make dolls the way they used to, not anymore.

Crawford waited another ten minutes until the noises had ceased, then calmly went next door, the light reflecting off the bare white walls. He kicked the shape on the floor.

No reaction.

He looked away in distaste. You never got used to it, even after all these years.

He slipped a pair of polythene shoe-covers over his feet and stepped over Hannah's body, fetching the mop and bucket. The blood pooled around her, and some of it had sprayed onto the walls. He filled the bucket with hot, soapy water from the metal sink and went to work.

As he did so, he whistled an old Elvis tune. What was it called? Ah, but he couldn't remember. One of the drawbacks of ageing — the ol' memory goes a bit haywire. Snapping on a pair of Marigolds, Crawford stooped and picked up the loose pieces, dropping them in extra-large freezer bags for safe disposal. A few fingers here and there, not too many. Her left breast was missing.

A souvenir, he supposed.

Her leg had been severely gnawed, stripped of flesh, and he lifted it, positioning the bleached white bone over his knee, pressing down hard with both hands. They were easier to dispose of in parts. He pushed, trying to snap it, but it wouldn't give. He was getting old. How much longer could he keep this up? In anger, he thrust his hands down and the femur shattered and Hannah jerked into life with a gurgled scream. He fell back, taken by surprise. She shielded her eyes from the light that burned her retinas, her mouth trying to open, straining against the fine cotton thread that bound it shut.

'What a mess,' he said, getting down on his hands and knees and squeezing Hannah's throat until he felt her windpipe crush beneath his fingers.

He stood and wiped the blood on his tweed trousers.

'What an absolute fucking mess.'

10

ELSPETH BUNCHED HER JACKET UP OVER HER HEAD TO SHIELD herself from the rain and hurried to her car, Robert's words ringing in her ears.

'There's a service station off the A9, about fifteen miles from here. I want everyone to go straight there. No buts. This is important.'

He had refused to say anymore.

Elspeth looked back, watching him get into the car with Laura. Deek, Aiden and Ted were already leaving in the big white rental van, their equipment still inside the manor. Had Robert gotten them an extra shooting day? Surely not.

She reached her old Fiat and tried to open the door, the rain soaking through her clothes. As usual, it was stuck. She jammed the button down with her thumb and shook the handle, but it wouldn't give.

Robert and Laura drove past her without a wave or a nod, and then she was alone. It was getting dark, and she felt unaccountably nervous. She rattled the handle, pulling hard, until it gave way and opened. She quickly entered, glad to be within the relative safety of the vehicle.

Feeling foolish, she laughed. It was perfectly safe out there too.

'You're being a real idiot, Elspeth.'

Glancing at the manor, she turned the key and the car spluttered into life. It was even more imposing after dark, the turrets piercing the night sky, the windows — every one of them shuttered by those wrought-iron bars — like so many insect eyes. And behind it, beyond the rocky precipice on which the manor balanced, miles and miles of ocean, the North Sea a suitably dramatic backdrop.

It made her want to slip into a silk gown and wander around with a candelabra, looking for Mr Rochester. All that was missing was a mad woman in the attic.

They had been lucky to get it, and now they had lost it. A whole day's footage rendered worthless, thanks in part to herself. No! She had to stop accepting blame. This was *all* on Robert. And Aiden. And Laura.

Anyone but yourself, eh?

She started up the driveway, the wipers struggling to keep up with the deluge. Far away, towards the mountains, lightning forked across the sky. As she drove, she checked her rear-view mirror. There was Robert's uncle at the front door, locking up, an umbrella in one hand, the porch light casting spidery shadows across his face.

Something caught her eye.

A light from a window, high up. She could have sworn it wasn't on just minutes before. Maybe he left lights on overnight to deter would-be burglars?

She parked by the side of the road and watched as Crawford's Land Rover pulled out of its parking space and headed down the driveway. He stopped parallel with her and wound down his window, motioning for Elspeth to do the same.

'Something wrong?' he shouted over the rain.

'No, just checking my phone.' Could he hear the nerves in her voice?

'No signal round these parts, and that's the way I like it.' He paused a moment, his eyes flicking back towards the house. Something in his expression changed, a brief flicker of emotion. 'You'd best be off now,' he said, his car idling alongside her.

'Sure. See you around. And thanks for letting us film today.' She smiled, put her foot down and drove away from him. As the car approached the forest, she glanced back one more time.

The attic light was off.

Behind her, Crawford's car stood guard.

She tried to laugh it off, but no laughter was forthcoming. Instead, a chill slithered up her spine, and then she was deep in the forest and the house fell from sight.

11

ELSPETH TURNED OFF THE MOTORWAY UNDER THE GLOW OF the golden arches and parked, running through the rain to McDonald's, where the rest of her crew sat waiting. They seemed in higher spirits than before, and she took an empty seat next to Robert.

'Thanks for coming,' he said through a mouthful of cheeseburger.

'This feels like an intervention.'

Robert laughed, wiping stray crumbs from his beard while Aiden noisily slurped on a Coke.

'Not quite. Though we do need to talk.'

'Can I order first?'

'Deek's getting you something right now. This can't wait. What took you so long, anyway?'

She looked over at the counter. Deek waited in line with Ted. They waved over to her, and she nodded back.

'I was talking to your uncle. Not a great conversationalist, is he?'

A shadowy look fell over Robert's face and he stopped chewing. 'What'd you talk about?'

'Nothing. I thought I saw a light on upstairs, that's all. Does that place have an attic?'

Robert ignored her question. 'You didn't tell him we'd left the equipment there, did you?'

'Of course not. So what's this all about? I'd kinda like to get home and go to bed.'

'How would you feel about a night shoot?'

The idea startled her. 'When? Tonight?'

'Sure. Why not?'

She stared at Robert, trying to gauge how serious he was. He stared back. 'But we've been shooting all day. You can't expect us to work for twenty-four hours.'

'You're right, I can't expect it. But I can hope you all feel the same way as me, and that's that without reshoots on location, we're hopelessly fucked. Is that how *you* feel, Elspeth?'

'I know I do,' interjected Laura, somewhat unnecessarily.

'I guess so, yeah,' said Elspeth. 'But how did you manage to convince your uncle? He never mentioned anything to me.'

Robert wiped his ketchup-stained hands on a napkin and tossed it to the floor.

'Well, I'm not sure *convinced* is the right word.'

She noticed that Aiden and Laura were suppressing grins. Something was up, and she needed to know what. Deek came over and placed a tray of fries and chicken nuggets in front of her. Without waiting for Robert to continue his halting, vague story, she tucked in to the fries. They tasted like they were sent from heaven, crispy and golden.

Robert let her enjoy the food for a moment, before continuing. 'What if I said I could get us in tonight?'

'I'd say you were lying.'

'He stole the keys!' announced Deek, unable to contain himself. Robert slapped him across the arm.

'Fuck man, I was just getting to that.'

Suddenly Elspeth lost her appetite. 'You what?'

Robert grinned a psychotic grin and pulled a keyring from the pocket of his leather jacket. The keys dangled, catching the rays of the fluorescent ceiling lights. He let them hang there like an out-of-work hypnotist, then snatched them back into his hand.

'Unfettered access.'

Aiden grinned too.

It must be contagious.

'All night long, baby,' said Aiden, before high-fiving Robert. Elspeth struggled to process this new development.

'But I watched him lock up.'

Robert pocketed the keys. 'Yeah, but this is the spare set. They were hanging in the kitchen.'

'So you stole them?'

Robert leaned back in his chair and looked down his nose at her. It was not a flattering angle. 'It's not stealing if you give them back,' he said, a little too smugly.

Laura nodded. 'It's borrowing. Plus, it's Robert's uncle. They're family. You can't steal from family, can you?'

Elspeth thought of just getting up and leaving, driving home to Aberdeen and dropping out of uni. Tonight. Right now. She could fire off an email to her tutor, make up some cock-and-bull excuse about a sick relative, and resit her final year next term. Without Robert. Without any of them.

But she didn't.

Because somewhere, deep down inside, she was intrigued.

She couldn't let it show.

'It's still breaking and entering,' she said.

'We're not breaking anything. We have the keys.'

'Yeah, Els,' said Deek. 'There's no one there overnight. He leaves with us at eight, and comes back at eight in the morning. I wonder what he does all night?'

'Probably out killing prostitutes,' said Elspeth.

Laura tried to steer them back on track. 'We can film all night, then pack up and be gone by half-seven. He'll never even know we were there.'

Elspeth popped a chicken nugget in her mouth and chewed thoughtfully.

'You're forgetting one thing though. We've no-one to film.'

'Well, that's not quite true, is it?' said Robert.

Elspeth felt four sets of eyes on her. Hungry. Greedy.

'Get to the point.'

'You've done some acting, haven't you?' asked Laura. As usual, the men had left it up to their spokesperson to deliver the news. They were too chickenshit to do it themselves.

'No,' she said firmly.

'You were in plays in high school.'

'I was third horse in my school production of *Oliver*, yes, but I hardly think that qualifies me.'

'But you said you were in a theatre group, yeah?'

'As costume designer, supposedly my role on *this* film, if the actresses ever wore any fucking clothes.' She pointed at Laura. 'Why don't *you* do it?'

'Because I'm not the one that told our lead actress to quit.'

Ah, there it is.

'Guys, don't put this on me. You were the ones that lied to her.'

'Well fuck's sake, Elspeth, what did she think?' said

Robert. 'You ever met a shy actress before? Unbelievable. And then you convinced her not to stay with all your feminist bullshit and basically fucked us all right up the arse.'

'Crude, Robert.'

'He's got a point,' piped up Aiden.

They were ganging up on her, crowding round like lions out for the kill. But she was no gazelle. She turned to Deek.

'What do you think?'

Deek looked anywhere but at her. He tore a salt sachet in half. 'I think...that if you don't do it, we're all going to fail uni. We won't have a film to show and we'll lose fifty percent of our grade.' He looked up at her and shrugged. 'Els, my mum'll kill me.'

'Wow,' muttered Elspeth. Deek averted his eyes.

'It's the least you could do,' said Aiden.

'If you're not going to do it for us, at least do it for yourself,' said Laura.

'It's this...or nothing,' said Robert.

Elspeth shook her head, disbelieving. She was all alone. This was bullshit! How could they even put her in this position? The situation was hardly her fault. *They* had tricked their actress into appearing nude, and somehow *she* was to blame? For helping a young girl to stand up for herself? Since when did that become a bad thing?

And yet the doubt lingered.

Maybe it *was* her fault? It was four against one. Was she too blind to see? Too arrogant?

No. She was in the right. She had sacrificed her own future for the sake of a woman's dignity.

She had also sacrificed her crew's futures.

Ted sat down next to them with a Diet Coke and fries. 'What'd I miss?' he asked.

'Nothing,' snapped Elspeth, before turning back to

Robert. 'It wouldn't be possible. It's too dark. We don't have time to film everything.'

Shit, that was weak. You've given them an in.

'No, but we could film enough. I'm talking one take for every scene, going flat out. You know the script by now, don't you?'

'Well...'

'Exactly. We film enough good stuff tonight, and it'll at least match with all the exterior shots we've got. Then next week, we cheat a bunch of angles, maybe have the climax take place at Rex's house instead of the manor.'

'We can do it,' said Laura. 'We can make it work. We can fix this. But it's all up to you. If you say no, then that's fine. We forget the whole thing, call it a night and go home.'

Manipulative bitch. That was a cheap, low blow.

'I won't do the nudity,' she said, shocked to hear the words stream out of her mouth. What the hell was she saying? Was she going to do this? She wasn't an actress.

Robert's eyes narrowed. He knew he had her on the end of the line and just needed to reel her in.

'We can discuss that.'

'No, Robert. I'm telling you now. Scrap the shower scene.' She made a face. Even thinking about it made her queasy. 'I'm not getting naked in front of you guys.'

You're my friends, she almost said. But they weren't, not really. Friends didn't make each other break into houses in the middle of the night and strip naked for some sordid, skeezy little movie.

'It's an important scene,' he said. He flinched and Elspeth assumed Laura had just kicked him under the table.

'I won't do it.'

'Elspeth, it's not for titillation, it's about Lacey washing away her fears.'

'It's about wanting to see my tits!' she shouted, slamming her fist on the table and making the empty drinks cartons jump. The other patrons looked around curiously, one couple shooting her a filthy look, the mother covering her toddler's ears.

She felt bad. Awful. She hated them all for putting her in this situation. She hated them, and yet somehow wanted to make it up to them.

It's not my fault, she told herself. So why didn't she believe it?

'I...I could do it in my underwear, I suppose,' she shrugged, surprised to hear herself say it.

Robert held up his hands in supplication. 'Fine. No nudity. Underwear only. It's a deal.'

She felt sick to her stomach. What had she just agreed to?

It's fine, you're a good-looking girl and you have a nice body. It's like being at the beach in a bikini. You've done that hundreds of times. If anything, your swimsuits are a lot more revealing than your underwear.

But it's not the same. There was something intimate about this. Private. They had no right. They couldn't make her. She looked at Laura.

If you're not going to do it for us, at least do it for yourself, she had said.

That's right. I'm not doing it for them. I'm doing it for myself.

But how many times would she have to lie to herself before she believed it?

A contented smile spread across Robert's lips, hidden by his thick beard.

'Okay then. If we're all in agreement, we're up against the clock. Finish up your food and let's go make some art.'

12

THE RAIN WAS GETTING HEAVIER AND ROBERT'S WIPERS struggled to keep up.

Trees blurred past the window, the headlights of the car picking out the white lines of the road and little else.

They passed a hitchhiker, the young woman trying to flag them down, but Robert drove by. Poor bitch. They didn't have time.

Laura rifled through the schedule.

'Right, it's gonna be tight, but I think we can do this.'

'That's what she said.'

She pretended not to hear. 'I suppose the whole stalking sequence is the most important. The phone call, the noises at the window. We need to get her waking up. Any insert shots of her hands we can leave and use the original footage. No one will notice. Basically, as much as we can get of her investigating the different rooms. And we can rewrite the last act to take place somewhere else, right?'

Robert frowned. 'I guess. It won't make sense, but we don't have a choice.' He was quiet a moment, thoughtful. It was unusual, and Laura felt it.

'What's up?' she asked.

'Should we scrap the shower scene?'

'I thought it was essential to the plot?'

Robert laughed. 'I suppose we could lose it. Elspeth's part of the crew, y'know. I don't want to humiliate her.'

Laura rested the notes on her lap. 'After the stunt she pulled today? She almost cost you the film, baby,' she purred.

Robert took his eyes off the road and searched his girlfriend's face for some hidden meaning. 'What are you saying? All of a sudden you *want* us to film the nudity?'

Laura cracked her knuckles. 'I'm just saying grow a pair of balls, Robert. Man up. If you want to have the scene, fucking film it. Don't let some bubble-headed bitch tell you what to do.'

'But she's our friend?'

'Friends don't ruin their friends' careers.'

'It sounds like you're punishing her.'

Laura took a long time to reply.

'That's exactly what we're going to do,' she finally said. 'That way, we're both happy. You get some tits for your movie and I get to put that snooty wee bitch in her place.'

They drove in silence for a while, hailstones pelting off the roof. A road sign shot by, the first hint of civilisation for miles.

'She'll have to do the sex scene with Ted next week,' said Robert. 'Isn't that enough?'

'Probably have to cut that,' said Laura. 'Doubt she'd be able to shag convincingly. She's a lesbian, isn't she?'

Robert smiled, warming to the idea. 'Hey, maybe you could take over from Ted. Might make it more convincing.'

'You'd like that, wouldn't you?'

'Sex sells, honey. Especially hot lesbo sex. Go on, take one for the team.'

'You're disgusting, you know that?'

Robert laughed. 'You honestly think you can talk her into it?'

'I've never met someone I couldn't manipulate,' smiled Laura.

'Apart from me.'

'Of course, baby,' said Laura, placing her hand on Robert's thigh and sliding it towards his crotch.

He breathed deeply and switched on the radio, filling the car with the hard rock of Thin Lizzy. The song took him back to his childhood, those nights lying in bed thinking about movies, sleep evading him like a restless phantom.

Laura was right. This was his *career* he was talking about, all he had ever wanted to do since the time his parents had bought a camcorder and eight-year-old Robert had corralled his friends into starring in his first motion picture, a seven-minute piece of garbage called *Attack of the Slug Men*.

How far had he really come?

The equipment was better, his cast and crew were (*marginally*) better, but sometimes he still felt like a kid, making dumb junk that only his parents would ever sit through. The idea made him feel sick and depressed.

He wondered if his heroes, Italian horror directors Dario Argento and Lucio Fulci, had ever encountered such doubts.

Not likely. But then, they didn't have to contend with do-gooders like Elspeth Murray, the girl sent from hell to sabotage his production. Wait, that wasn't true. Elspeth was his friend, and she was only trying to—

Laura's hand found Robert's erection and lightly

squeezed it through his boxers. His muscles tightened as she worked it free.

'Slow down,' she said. 'It's dangerous driving at night.'

He believed Laura could do it. She was the only one of them that would be able to convince — or coerce — Elspeth into a nude scene. Thank goodness he was immune to Laura's manipulative games, he thought, as she traced her finger up his shaft and he bit his lip and forgot what they had even been talking about.

Elspeth took the turnoff from the main road and guided the Fiat down the track, taking it slow. The drive was very different at night.

Sometimes, in the darkness, the greatest thing to fear is your own mind.

It likes to play tricks.

She narrowed her eyes and stopped the car, checking the last message she had sent, back in the McDonald's car park.

It was to Sandy.

> Hey, please call me. We're filming overnight, and I made our actress leave and now I'm in the lead role and they're making me take my clothes off. I'm scared but I think I have to. I'm sorry. X

It was unread. Elspeth checked the time. It was coming up for nine. Sandy would still be at the gym.

Well, it was too late now. The signal was gone. Sandy couldn't help her. No one could.

Except yourself.

She started the car again, heading for the manor, pulling in next to the white rental van.

Déjà vu, huh?

She got out, bracing herself against the sea wind that battered the cliffs mere yards from where she stood. In the distance, further up the coastline, an old lighthouse stood watch, the only light for miles around, apart from the stars that twinkled in obsidian solitude.

There was no sign of life in the manor.

Robert, Laura and Ted waited on the porch, Robert chain-smoking his Marlboros like he was trying to get rid of evidence, Laura poring over the script like the dutiful producer she was.

Elspeth wondered if he would want to start with the shower scene.

Not that she would be stripping off. Not all the way. Her stomach dropped just thinking about it. Her whole class would see. Her tutors. Her *parents*, for god's sake.

Shouldn't have had those chicken nuggets.

Aiden got out of the van next to her, fiddling with the camera and together they headed for the shelter of the porch. Deek stood by the cliff edge, headphones on, holding the boom mic out over the waves.

'He gonna jump?' Elspeth asked Aiden. 'I might join him.'

Aiden shrugged. 'Getting some ambient tracks. I think he's learnt from experience that we usually overdub most of Rob's movies.'

'Maybe if the director wouldn't talk all through the shots, we wouldn't have to.'

'Maybe if he, y'know, hired real actors.'

Elspeth raised her eyebrows. 'Yeah, well I guess you're stuck with me this time.'

Aiden lifted the camera to his eye and stared through the viewfinder at her. 'Damn right. Get ready for your closeup.'

She gave him the finger.

'Aiden, go and get Deek. Let's get on with this.' She left Aiden and carried on towards the porch. 'And stop filming my arse,' she said without turning back.

Aiden twisted the dial to keep focus on her tight jeans.

'You love it,' he shouted. He panned over to the ancient pine forest and beyond that, the mountains, the camera losing focus in the darkness.

They were pretty alone out here.

Pretty damn alone.

Robert waited with typical flair until they were all gathered together on the porch. Then, he slid the key in the lock and slowly — more for dramatic effect than anything — turned it. The lock was stiff, but it gave way. One hefty *click*, and the door opened.

Elspeth leaned back against the railing, trying to remind herself why they were doing this, as Robert's words skipped through her head.

It's not stealing, it's borrowing.

Like hell. This was a breaking and entering, and they all knew it, all of them now privy to a crime. Accessories. But no one was going to get hurt, were they? If it was indeed a crime, then it was a victimless one.

'Ladies and jellyspoons,' announced Robert theatrically. He paused. 'Let's do this.'

With that flourish out of the way, he stepped across the perimeter. Only once inside did it become real. A crime had now officially been committed.

'We've got a lot of work to do. Is there any equipment we need from the cars? If so, get it now, I don't want to be hanging around waiting. Deek, you all set?'

'Aye.'

'Aiden?'

'Damn straight, my man.'

'Then let's go shoot this fucker. What scene, Laura?'

She checked her notes. 'I figured we should start with the stalking sequence.'

Elspeth breathed a sigh of relief, a small weight lifted from her shoulders. That meant her big scene wouldn't be shot until later.

'I'm gonna go change,' she said. She hoped the costume would fit. It should, her and Hannah were a similar build and height. She looked down the long, dark corridor towards the staircase. It was further than she remembered, and the lights were off, the switch way down the hall. She could make out the bottom few steps and no more.

'I'll come with you,' said Aiden. 'Get the camera.'

Elspeth wasn't sure if it was for her benefit or his, and didn't care either way. Safety in numbers and all that. This place was creepy after dark. Things that had seemed flamboyant or campy during the day were now strange and otherworldly. Shadows cast by the porch light broke across the walls, twisted and sinuous, a maze with no exit.

Together they walked, stepping from rug to wooden flooring and back again, reminding Elspeth of the little boy with the tricycle in *The Shining*. It was the last thing she wanted to think about right now. They came to the light switch, and she flicked it on. It did little to assuage her trep-idation.

She wanted to speak, but could think of nothing worth-while to say, so instead the pair climbed the stairs, reached the top and went their separate ways, Elspeth to the actors' bedroom, Aiden to the camera storeroom.

'If you need me, I'll be in the next room,' said Aiden as he left her by the half-open door. It was an odd thing to say, and they both knew it.

'Thanks,' said Elspeth, doing her best to ignore the palpable awkwardness.

Aiden waited for her to say something else, then nodded, turned and carried on.

She entered the room, careful not to let the door close until she found the light, lest a hand reach out from under the bed and grab her.

She took out her iPhone and opened the Music app, hitting shuffle. The first song that came on was *Somebody's Watching Me* by Rockwell.

'Not right now,' she said, and skipped to the next track.

Robert waited with Laura, Ted and Deek. He turned to the soundman and said, 'We won't need audio for most of these shots. It'll just slow us down. Dialogue scenes only.'

Deek nodded, secretly pleased. 'No problem, man. I'll get some ambient tracks or something.'

'Good idea.' When Deek didn't move, Robert tried again. 'So what are you waiting for?'

'Oh, you mean now? By myself? In the dark?'

Robert looked at him like Deek was the world's biggest idiot. 'Put the lights on.'

Embarrassed, Deek shuffled out of earshot, heading for the storage room at the top of the stairs.

'What about me?' said Ted.

Robert didn't know, so let Laura answer.

'Go wait somewhere, and keep out of the way.'

'Can't I just go home?'

'You got a car?'

'No,' he sighed.

'Then read the script or something. We'll drive you back when we're ready. Now go, we don't have time for this.'

Ted looked like he was about to say something, then stopped himself. Shoving his hands in his pockets, he trudged down the hallway and out of sight. When he was a safe distance away, Robert locked the front door.

'What are you doing?' asked Laura.

'I've already had one actress bail on us today. Can't have a second.'

'So you're locking us all in? They're not gonna like it.'

'They're not gonna know.'

'Rob, *I* don't like it. It's a fire hazard.' She pulled a sheet out from her file. 'It's right here in the Risk Assessment.'

'Fuck the Risk Assessment. Here, if it makes you feel any better, *you* take the key.'

He held it out for her and she cautiously reached for it, half expecting him to rescind his offer. He didn't, and she plucked the brass keyring from his open palm. It was heavier than it looked, old and rusted. Her dress had no pockets, so she tucked it into her bra.

'Now no one leaves unless you say so,' he said, smiling mirthlessly at her.

In the dark, it looked like a sneer.

THIRTEEN MILES AWAY, CLAIRE BRUEGEL HUGGED HER PARKA close as the rain soaked through to her sweater. The sun had long-since dipped below the trees, and only darkness remained.

Shit.

She was in trouble now. Only two cars had passed in the last hour, and neither had stopped to pick her up. She looked over her shoulder at her bright red pack, sheltered in the woods beneath a pine tree. At least, she *hoped* it was sheltered.

Headlights crested the hill. She wiped her hair from her face, trying to make herself look presentable. As a hitch-hiker, she wanted to strike the balance between demure and sexy. Demure in case it was a woman driver, and sexy for the men. The men were always more likely to pick up a young, attractive woman.

She ran to her pack and grabbed her sign, EDIN-BURGH scrawled in black marker across the scrap of increasingly soggy cardboard. She held it out and stepped to the edge of the road, the rain battering her face. The car was getting closer. Would it stop? It didn't seem to be slowing.

'Hey!' she shouted, as the car roared past, deliberately swerving into a puddle and showering her with water.

'Bastard!' she screamed, though she knew he couldn't hear her. 'I hope you crash!'

And then it was quiet again, except for the heavy droplets splashing in the puddles and the wind howling its mournful wail through the trees. Was she gonna be stuck here all night, with no tent, no shelter, and no food? She thought about her father back home. He must be ill with worry. She laughed drily.

That bastard. That cruel, sick fuck.

He had gone too far this time. She was used to his comments as he leered at her over his copy of *The Daily Mail*, the stench of whiskey on his breath as he insisted on hugging her goodbye every morning, the way his erection pressed against her through his filthy grey jogging bottoms.

She hated him. She wanted him dead.

Last night had been the final straw.

She came home from school late. Detention. Nothing serious, just texting in class. Only problem, she was texting about Miss Frank. Miss Frank had been none too pleased when she snatched Claire's phone from her hand and perused the missive. It was fair to say that the message had not been complimentary of Miss Frank's weight.

An hour of detention. No problem. Her father would be at work til six. He'd never have to know.

So when Claire arrived home and found the front door half-open, she was concerned.

'Get in here,' Carl Bruegel slurred from the kitchen. She did as he asked, fearful of the consequences of not following her father's orders. He leaned against the counter, sweat staining his pits. 'Where've you been?' The room stank of booze, the stench emanating from his pores.

'Studying,' she stammered.

'Aye, bollocks, like. Studying some wee cunt's cock, aye?'

'Dad, no.'

'Yer ma ne'er raised ye tae be a slag.'

Yeah, but that's not why she left us, is it, you abusive fuck?

She bit her tongue. If only her mother had taken her with her when *she* escaped. Why hadn't she? Claire's eyes stung from the oncoming tears. No, she wouldn't cry, not for this waste of space. She was sixteen, a grown woman. Soon she would graduate and leave school, leave home, leave this monster that called itself her father far behind.

Some things are best left forgotten.

'Come here,' he said, his eyes crossing.

'No.'

'Dinnae disobey me ya hoor. Yer nae too old to be dishi... dishi...dishiplined.' He took a step towards her and almost overbalanced.

'Leave me alone,' she said, backing up.

'Aye, yer nae tae old fae me to skelp yer arse. Aye, fuckin' skelp yer wee bare arse.' He smiled at the thought and Claire felt bile rising in her throat.

'You stay away from me. *Please*. I'm sixteen, you can't do this. I'm an adult now.'

His worn belt slithered out between his hands and he pulled it taut, the leather snapping together with a sound that made her jump. He smacked the belt off the sink, sending a couple of dirty plates crashing to the linoleum.

'See what you did,' he spat, his bloodshot eyes finding

hers. He lunged forwards and Claire found herself pressed up against the wall, his breath strong enough to melt steel. He took her by the shoulders and threw her to the side, her face bashing into the fridge. She slid onto the cool linoleum floor, legs splayed. Blood ran from her nose.

Claire screamed, but screaming was no use. The first time this had happened, the neighbours had heard and called the police. The second time, they hadn't bothered. Not the third, nor the fourth. Not ever again. She wondered if her dad had paid them a visit.

Carl Bruegel raised the belt high and brought it down with practiced efficiency.

Now, standing by the side of a desolate country road, she shook at the memory. Her arms ached, blood seeping through the rudimentary bandages. Her shoulders and breasts were a patchwork of bruises and lacerations.

'You bastard,' she said as the pine trees rustled in the wind.

Then lights, *headlights*, coming her way. She choked back tears and held out her sign again. Surely this one would stop. Someone had to. She was due some good luck, a respite from the unremitting misery of life.

'Please stop, please stop, please stop,' she chanted like a mantra.

The car sped towards her. Was it her imagination, or was it slowing?

No, it wasn't. In fact, it was speeding up and heading straight for her.

She only had a second to react.

She needed more time.

Claire leapt out of the way, but the car caught her trailing ankle, sending her spinning away from the road and hurtling into a ditch. She tried to get to her feet, but the pain was immense. She looked and saw her foot hanging limply, the bone broken.

The car rolled to a stop, the door opening, someone getting out. Maybe he hadn't seen her?

'Help,' she called out.

She lay on the grassy verge, waiting, unable to move. He walked unhurriedly, coming to help, to drive her to the nearest hospital. She couldn't blame him for not seeing her. She should have worn a brighter jacket; the navy parka would be hard to spot in the darkness.

As he walked steadily towards her, the moonlight glinted off something in his hand.

A butcher's knife.

Claire's heart skipped a beat, then another.

'Oh shit. Oh fuck!'

She scrambled through the grass towards the imposing forest, clawing her fingers into the dirt, pulling herself along, not daring to look back, her survival instinct kicking in. She stood on her one good leg and tried hopping from tree to tree. Panicking, she lowered her foot and put weight on it, collapsing face-first onto the forest bed.

Footsteps crackled behind her, snapping twigs and crushing pine cones underfoot. She dragged herself onwards. Disappearing into the forest was her only chance. She had a mad vision of her father bearing down on her, the leather belt wrapped around his fist, his fly unzipped.

Then she felt a hand on her hair, lifting her up into a kneeling position. A heavy work-boot came down hard on her broken ankle and she screamed in agony, the pain flaring through her body. She heard the bone crunch as the boot ground down against her.

'Scream all you want,' said a weary voice. 'There's no one around for miles.'

A rough hand gripped her beneath the chin, pulling her backwards, her torso bending at an unnatural angle. She felt a great pressure in her stomach as her internal organs pressed against one another, cutting off her oxygen supply.

Just use the knife. Use the fucking knife and get it over with.

She was so far back now she could see her attacker, his face silhouetted against the moon. She was surprised to find it wasn't her father.

The man raised the knife and plunged it into Claire's throat, the razor-edged blade sliding in easily, puncturing the soft flesh of her jugular. Her vision blurred and for a moment she smiled.

There has to be a better life than this, she thought, and then the blade was rudely withdrawn and hot blood bubbled up from the wound, her lifeless body slumping down among the bed of pine needles.

Ross Crawford wiped the bloody implement on a tuft of grass. He gazed down at the body, then went back to his car to fetch the black plastic bin-liners.

His work for the night was just beginning.

Fun, Fun, Fun by The Beach Boys.

Perfect.

What better way to banish a creepy atmosphere than with five Californian teenagers singing about a fast car. Elspeth felt relaxed. At ease. It was absurd, really. She had no reason to be scared. There's just something about big houses, particularly unfamiliar ones...

Too many corners, too many doors. Too much space and not enough light.

Too many places to hide.

She focused on Brian Wilson's falsetto vocal tag, and lifted the blouse and faded jeans from the floor, where Hannah had left them.

Hannah. She wondered if the girl was home now, and wished she'd asked Mr Crawford. She hoped Hannah didn't regret her decision.

If she was still here, you wouldn't be in this situation.

That was true. But at least she hadn't compromised her morals. Well, apart from breaking into a house and getting ready to strip off for a student film. The more she thought about it, the more confused and annoyed she got. How had events spiralled out of control to this extent? How had she let herself be bullied and cajoled into this? She held up the blouse. It was so flimsy it was almost transparent.

You got yourself into this, now get yourself out.

She took off her vest and laid it on the bed. The Beach Boys gave way to Bowie as she undressed.

The battery died, the music cutting out.

She heard a thud and dropped the blouse in surprise, turning in the direction of the noise.

'Aiden? That you?'

No, it couldn't be. Aiden was in the adjacent room. That noise had come from the wall with the window on it.

The exterior wall.

She shuffled her way to the window and looked out through the iron bars. Below was a sheer drop of hundreds of feet, from the second-floor window all the way down to the waves that pounded the rocks at the bottom of the cliff. There was nothing on the other side of that wall. Nothing. She couldn't understand where the sound had come from. A seagull flying into the side of the building? No, that was stupid. She backed away from the window, suddenly feeling very exposed.

Aiden breathed a sigh of relief.

That was too close.

Crammed into the confines of the crawlspace between the walls, there was barely enough space to turn his head, never mind lurch towards the peephole. He angled his body, sucked in a deep breath, and peered at Elspeth through the small hole as she stood in her underwear, unaware of his presence.

The passageway was his own little secret.

He had discovered it that morning. In a rare stroke of good fortune, he had selected a bedroom at the far-end of the hallway to be the designated storeroom, and was unpacking the Dedolights and putting them in the massive walk-in closet when he noticed one of the panels looked rather fragile. On closer inspection, it had given way and led into the crawlspace, giving him access to every room on one side of the upper floor. Each room had a hole drilled into the wall, sometimes two. All he had to do was crawl beneath the windows and he could spy on roughly a quarter of Crawford Manor. He wasn't surprised. These old buildings were chock full of weird hidden passageways and shit.

It also gave him an appreciation for Mr Crawford. The man was a voyeur, which made him a kindred spirit. After all, Aiden was a cinematographer, and what was that but a glorified title for someone who likes to watch?

He had already spied on Hannah this morning, and had planned to be here again at the end of night, but fate conspired against him on that one. Never mind, he could always jerk off to the footage at home. Robert would want a copy too, no doubt.

But now this unexpected delight!

Elspeth.

Everyone had fancied her at some point during uni. As far as he knew though, she hadn't dated anyone during the last four years. Apparently she was a lesbian, or so the rumour went. He didn't know if it was true or not, but he was sure of one thing — that this was as close as *he* would ever get to her.

Elspeth Murray, in the flesh, and only ten feet away from him.

He could almost smell her.

His knee thumped off the wall and she looked his way again.

She seemed to be staring right at him. He bit down hard on his lip, afraid to move.

It's just the rats in the walls, my dear.

She took a step forwards. Had she spotted the peephole?

No, she was looking around. She shook her head and walked to the bed, hurriedly throwing on the blouse and jeans as Aiden watched.

Elspeth gathered up her belongings, took one last look at the wall, then unlocked the door and left the room as Aiden shuffled his way back towards the storeroom. The others would be looking for him. He smiled, thinking of Hannah and then Elspeth.

It had been a good day all round.

15

Sandy Beaumont arrived home to an empty flat just before nine, her heart beating a little faster than normal. Elspeth wasn't back yet, and that was good. She didn't want to be caught in a lie.

Sandy had foregone the gym. There was something more important for her to do on this grotty, rainy Friday night. She removed a small parcel from her pocket and placed it on the table, then hung her jacket on the radiator to dry. She looked at the parcel for a while, daring herself to open it, to take another look.

No, not yet. Shower first.

She stripped off her gym clothes — she had changed into them in case Elspeth had come home early — and headed for the shower, the noise of the water obscuring the ringing of her phone in the living room.

She stepped out, dried her long blonde hair and wrapped a towel around her head. It was half-past nine, and she expected Elspeth any time now.

Sandy smiled. She felt better now, the way hot showers on cold winter nights always made her feel, and padded barefoot over to the table. The parcel was small, and she undid the little bow and opened it. Inside was a velvet box.

She didn't *need* to look. She knew exactly what was in there. She had been eyeing it through the jewellery shop window for over a month now.

A ring. Platinum, with a single diamond set into it. She took the ring out and held it, thought about placing it on her own finger. It would fit, she figured, but somehow that seemed wrong, a betrayal. This wasn't for her. This was for Elspeth. She put the engagement ring back in the box.

'Maybe tonight,' she mused. 'Or maybe not.' She grinned, the kind that shows off all your teeth and makes passers-by think you're insane.

She was sure Elspeth would say yes. Positive. Absolutely convinced. The only reason she hadn't asked yet was because she might say no. Not that she *would* say no. She would say yes. Definitely. Why not? Probably.

Sandy realised her toes were clenched so tight she was about to give herself a cramp. She carried the box through to the bedroom like it was a bomb and opened a drawer. She tucked it into a sock, then balled that one up inside another.

No, not tonight. It can wait. It has to be special.

She had to be sure.

It was coming up for ten when Sandy Beaumont checked her phone. She saw the missed calls from Elspeth, read the text, once, twice, over and over until it started to make sense. She rang back, going straight to voicemail. She told Elspeth to call her, to get the fuck out, to stop and think about what was happening.

By ten-fifteen, she knew she wasn't getting a reply.

By ten-twenty, she had decided to find her, to bring her home.

There was only one problem, but it was a pretty insur-mountable one — she had no idea where Elspeth was.

An old house in the country was all she knew. Near the sea, as if that narrowed it down.

'Shit!' shouted the girl, as she rummaged through Elspeth's notes and folders, looking for information on the shoot. She opened her girlfriend's laptop and checked the desktop, searching for folders or files or anything. She clicked open the internet.

Then she had an idea.

16

'HELLO? WHO IS THIS?'

Elspeth clutched the receiver of the old-school dial-up phone. It felt strangely nostalgic, taking her back to her childhood, when she had sat in the hallway chatting to friends on the communal phone, her mother hovering by the doorway and listening in, making sure she wasn't talking to any boys. This particular one she had picked up on eBay for the princely sum of £4.99. As far as she could tell, Mr Crawford didn't have a phone in the house.

'Please stop calling me. This isn't funny anymore.'

The boom mic hovered inches from her face like a miniature zeppelin and she wondered how it wasn't in shot.

'Listen, my boyfriend will be back any minute now.' She gasped. 'How do you know I don't have a boyfriend? Because you watch me every night? Oh my god!'

She slammed the receiver down and gazed into the ether.

'It can't be Rex,' she said. 'He's been dead for two years. Unless he's calling...from beyond the grave?'

Someone behind the camera giggled. Probably Deek. Robert shot him a look.

Elspeth continued her monologue. 'I suppose it has been two years to the day. What if he's come back to haunt me? What if he's come back...to seek revenge?'

As Elspeth spoke, she was reminded of an old Harrison Ford quote regarding the script for *Star Wars*.

You can type this shit, but you can't say it.

And to think she had been worried about her underwear scene. Now she was more concerned about being laughed off the screen for her delivery of Robert's preposterous dialogue.

'Aaaaaand cut. That was good, Elspeth. Great, in fact. Just the right level of fear. Let's move on. Laura, what's next?'

'You don't want to go again?' asked Elspeth.

Robert waved a hand dismissively. 'No, that was fine. We gotta keep going, it's almost midnight already.'

Laura scored through another scene in the script. Her eyes scanned the pages. 'Okay, maybe five or six shots following her around the house.'

'Shit,' said Aiden. 'We need the dolly track.'

'So?'

'So, it's upstairs.'

The dolly, a tripod mounted on rails, allowed for smooth and steady tracking shots. It was essential for creating a professional looking film, so when Robert shook his head and said, 'Forget it,' no one was surprised.

'Look Rob, I know we don't have much time, but I can't shoot it handheld on the Canon. It'll look like shit.'

'No choice. It takes too long. Just put a wide-angle lens on. It'll add verisimilitude.'

'It'll add motion sickness.'

'Even better,' he replied, only half-listening. 'Deek, we'll shoot this stuff MOS.'

'Okay,' said Deek, his voice uncertain.

Robert stared at him. 'MOS means without sound, dumbass. So go wait upstairs or something, you'll just get in the way.'

Sighing, Deek grabbed his equipment and headed up the stairs.

Elspeth watched him go, almost feeling sorry for the boy, for the way Robert treated him. Then she remembered how he had failed to stand up for her in McDonald's and turned her back on him.

Fuck him.

She had no friends here.

~

Deek Gareth — only his mother called him Derek — waited at the top of the stairs, deciding what to do next. He wandered down the corridor to where it split into a T-shape, each branch leading off to different areas of the house.

He yawned and stretched and thought about just lying down and having a snooze. He had been up since six this morning. That meant he'd been awake for...fifteen hours? Seventeen? More? He was too tired to count, but knew he couldn't risk sleeping. What if Robert found him and shouted at him in front of everyone? In front of Elspeth?

Oh Elspeth. He felt bad for her. Was it partly his fault? He didn't think so, yet Elspeth was acting like it was. He had done nothing wrong, had taken no sides. Okay, so he could have done more to help her, but sometimes it's better just to go with the flow. Deek didn't want to ruffle any feathers. He was no good at confrontation. He recalled the time Robert had made him cry on the set of *Burns Night*. Robert had chewed him out in front of everyone, and they had all laughed at him, even the topless girl playing one of the victims. She had pointed and laughed harder than anyone. Deek still remembered the weird mixture of shame and arousal. Come to think of it, the only person who hadn't laughed had been Elspeth. She had followed him, comforted him.

Maybe he should have said something. He still could...? Ah, it was fine. She could handle herself. It was none of his business.

He thought about trying to find Ted, then decided against it. He hated actors, they were so self-absorbed, so vain, always taking selfies and fixing their hair in the mirror.

With nothing else to do, he switched on his equipment and adjusted the dials on the recorder, choosing the left-hand path and strolling down the hallway. It was the same as all the rest. Paintings adorned the walls, noblemen and women and aristocrats, often posing with their faithful hounds. He paused before one and squinted at it.

Was that Mr Crawford? Surely not. He looked so...so *young*. At twenty-one, Deek had a hard time imagining any old person ever being young, just as he had no concept of himself ageing.

'Getting old is for old people,' he would say without a trace of irony.

But that sure looked like Mr Crawford. The grim expression gave him away. Beside him sat a beautiful woman, auburn hair tumbling over her shoulders, her face vital and alive. Was that his wife? She was a babe. In fact, she looked a little like Elspeth. Deek was impressed.

There was hope for him yet.

In her lap, she cradled something. A baby? It was hard to tell. The bundle was odd, too large and misshapen. Engraved on the frame were the words *HARRIET'S ARRIVAL*. Deek shrugged and moved on.

The painting next to it was missing, the wallpaper where it had once hung noticeably less faded.

To Deek, a simple boy, the details had no real significance. He placed the sound-isolating Sennheiser headphones over his ears, enjoying the blessed silence, then unscrewed the boom mic from its pole and carried it handheld. Might as well get some ambient soundtracks. It was an essential job, helping to cover awkward edits due to the variance of sound tones within a single room. Just by moving the boom a few inches, the audio could pick up a new buzz or hiss that could be a nightmare in the edit. He pointed the mic down the corridor and held still. Thirty seconds was usually sufficient, and easy to loop.

He walked into the nearest room, another unused bedroom. How many bedrooms did one old bastard need?

In this room, he picked up a slight buzzing. He swung the mic, the sound increasing until he was pointing right at it. An electrical socket. It usually was. He recorded it, taking the time to peer around the room. They all blended into each other after a while. Fancy shit, expensive looking, sitting here going to waste, untouched and unloved.

Like my dick, he thought, and laughed, ruining the recording.

Outside the seagulls cawed. He hit pause and went to the window, pulling open the heavy velvet drapes.

'So fucking weird,' he whispered.

Like the rest, these windows were blocked off by iron

bars. He gazed out between them, at the vast expanse of sea. Actually, maybe the bars made sense, at least on the cliff-facing side of the mansion. You wouldn't want any kids falling out of the windows. Ain't nobody gonna survive *that* fall. He wondered if Mr Crawford had any kids, and decided to ask Robert sometime. Not tonight, though. They were too busy.

Faint footsteps marched through his headphones. Someone was coming. He directed the mic towards the door, searching for the source, but it made little difference. He aimed the boom mic down, the footsteps decreasing in volume.

Odd. They couldn't be coming from above him. Unless...

Deek pointed the mic at the ceiling and a chill ran through him. He was right. They *were* coming from above. But there wasn't a third floor, was there?

No, but there might be an attic. Don't be such a wee feardy!

But then, who was up there? Wasn't everyone downstairs filming? Could it be Ted? No, he was down there too. They all were.

'Hannah?' he squeaked.

The footsteps stopped directly over him. Deek waited. He thought he could detect a faint shuffling and cranked the dial up to ten.

Breathing.

That's what it was. An asthmatic panting sound, like a sick dog.

He walked towards the door, mic pointing at the ceiling, and the sound followed.

What the actual fuck?

He took the headphones off and listened. Nothing. He stepped out into the hallway, then replaced the 'phones. The breathing was still there.

'Guys?' said Deek, barely recognising his own voice. He took a few steps one way, then a few the other. 'Who's there?'

He walked down the hallway, the dreadful sound keeping pace, Deek gaining speed without even realising it until he was jogging, the breathing and shuffling following him all the way down.

What is *that?*

He would come to the corner in a moment. What if there was something waiting for him? His bladder was full and he was afraid he might piss himself.

A voice, he thought he could hear a voice, muttering, mumbling, slurring. Was it laughing at him?

He rounded the corner and there it was, a dark shape in front of him. He closed his eyes and crashed right into it. Deek screamed.

Elspeth, in turn, also screamed, as Deek clattered into her.

The noise almost split Deek's skull in two. He threw off the headphones and turned the dial back down to three.

'What the fuck, Elspeth, don't sneak up on me like that!'

Elspeth put a hand to her heart.

'Sorry,' she gasped, 'I didn't know you were so easy to scare.' She looked hard at Deek. 'You okay? You're pale as fu—'

'I'm fine,' he said, answering too quickly. 'You just gave me a wee fright, that's all.'

'I'll say. Jesus. Listen, Robert's looking for you. We're doing audio stuff now.'

'Okay, I'll be right down,' he said, turning away from her to hide the small, dark patch of urine on his jeans.

Deek cast one last nervous glance up at the ceiling. No way was he going to tell anyone about this. He'd never hear the end of it. The sound man, frightened by a scary noise. So scared he peed himself.

He switched the recorder off and skulked down the stairs behind Elspeth.

The thing in the attic watched them until they disappeared.

17

TED REILLY WAS BORED.

The insufferable tedium of being on set was one thing drama school hadn't prepared him for. He could have just gone home, for goodness' sake. He had filmed his scenes already, and now he had to reshoot some of them because Hannah had walked. He bit idly at the skin on his fingers, then stopped himself. It wouldn't do to have an actor with bleeding fingers. He had an image to maintain, had to look his best at all times, even his hands. No part of an actor's body was safe. Nothing was private, nor off-limits. On Tuesday they would shoot the sex scene, and Robert had informed him that full nudity was required.

It would not be a problem. Ted looked after himself. He had to. An out-of-shape actor is an out-of-work actor, which is why he was booked in for a back, sack and crack the day before the sex scene.

He yawned, he leaned, he scratched. He stood, he paced, he thought, all the while Robert fawned over Elspeth, encouraging her, sweet-talking her.

She's actually not bad, thought Ted, *considering the circumstances. Better than Hannah, anyway.*

Ted was no fool. He recognised the script's shortcomings, knew bad dialogue when he saw it. He spotted plot holes big enough to drive a double-decker bus through, and characterisation that was, at best, paper-thin. But he also knew it was the lead role in a film.

Rex Carmichael, husband from beyond the grave.

As beginnings to a career went, it was inauspicious. He imagined being on Graham Norton's chat show in a few years, squirming in embarrassment as Graham screened a clip of the long-forgotten movie and Ted graciously accepted the laughs from the audience, deflating the tension with a deliciously timed zinger. He tried to think of one, but couldn't. God, he was tired!

He sidled up to Laura as they waited between takes, Aiden trying to hurriedly put together a lighting set-up as Elspeth sat patiently reading the script.

'Do you still need me?' he asked the producer.

Laura studied her notes and replied without even looking at him. Ted hated the way she did that. 'Yeah, we've got the argument coming up soon, then you're done,' she said with total disinterest.

'Can't you just use the footage from earlier and cut around it?'

She looked up at him with undisguised annoyance. 'It was a two-shot. There's no way to remove Hannah unless we do a digital zoom.' She gave him a sideways glance. 'You want to look like a bunch of pixels?'

Ted shook his head as Laura went back to her notes, scoring through scenes with her trusty yellow highlighter.

'Aiden, hurry it up,' she said as Ted crept away from her and left the room.

Fuck it, he had to sleep, unless they wanted their handsome leading man to have bags under his eyes. If they needed him, they could bloody well come and find him. He wandered out into the hallway and headed up the stairs to the bedrooms.

What time was it?

Ted liked to be in bed by ten most nights. A full nine hours sleep was *essential* to maintaining a clear complexion. How did they expect him to look his best for Tuesday's shoot without a full nine hours? What were they, monsters?

He entered the actors' room and threw himself down on the bed, the duvet enveloping him, welcoming him into its soft warmth. Fully clothed, he closed his eyes and waited for sleep to carry him off.

Soon, he was drifting, heedless of the sounds in the corner, that strange muffled breathing. He assumed it was all part of his dream. Within minutes, Ted was dead to the world.

He didn't hear the awkward, shuffling footsteps, one heavier than the other, nor smell the malodorous stench that emanated from the obscene mass shambling across the room towards him.

He wasn't kidding about needing that full nine hours.

He stirred when something climbed into bed with him.

'Mmmmm,' he said.

It was the breathing that finally alerted him. Hot and wet, like a beast in heat, but slow, real slow.

Ted gradually came to, his eyelids fighting to stay closed. He could hear the exhalations, feel them on his nape. An arm reached around, spooning him. The sensation was not altogether unpleasant.

'Hannah?' he said, still half-asleep. 'That you? Is it my time to film?'

Something touched the back of his neck.

Lips. Dry, cracked lips. They opened, and ragged, sharp teeth traced his soft, actorly skin.

'Hey, stop that,' he murmured, wishing for another ten minutes, just another ten minutes in bed, was that too much to ask? He liked Hannah, she was very pretty, but he already had a girlfriend. If she was trying to sleep with him, she was barking up the wrong tree.

The hand closed over his own, the coarse skin rubbing against him and Ted snapped to attention.

That was not Hannah's hand.

'Jesus, who is this?' he said, shifting his weight and turning round to face his bedmate.

In the darkness, he could only make out the eyes, two clouded marbles deeply set into a creased, patchwork face. It lunged forwards, ragged lips closing over his own, a brittle tongue worming its way inside his mouth. Ted gagged as hands clamped themselves to the sides of his head, pulling him against the foul thing in the bed. It kissed him.

It was like kissing a grave.

He kicked out but it wrapped itself around his legs, holding him close, cocooning him in its foul body, and then it wasn't kissing, it was *biting*, broken teeth sinking into the soft pink of his tongue and tearing it free, his mouth filling with blood. Ted tried to muscle his way loose, but his arms were pinned. The ghastly mouth bit down on his teeth, enamel grinding against enamel, until he heard them — *felt* them — crack, splintering into his gums.

His whole body shook in agony.

Soon, he shook no more.

18

Sandy kept checking her phone, but there was nothing from Elspeth. No messages, no calls. She was down to one bar of signal, and her internet had gone from 4G to 3G to that weird symbol that seemed to promise internet access without ever delivering on it.

The headlights of a passing car glanced across her face. Beside her, in the driver's seat, sat Gordon Gunn, Elspeth's classmate and friend, a look of grim determination etched onto his boyish features.

'You really think she's in trouble?' he asked.

'Yeah. You saw the message.'

Gordon clenched his jaw. 'It's not like her. She wouldn't do something she didn't want to.'

'I know. And that's why we're going to go get her.'

Gordon nodded. He had received a Facebook message from Sandy an hour ago, sent via Elspeth's account. He had, naturally, checked it immediately. Sandy had counted on the fact. She knew Gordon fancied her girlfriend, and would do anything for her. You could tell by the way he always commented on her photos, the way he liked every status update. Sandy didn't mind. In fact, she rather enjoyed how all the boys were after Elspeth, not knowing she preferred more feminine company.

He had taken no convincing. As soon as Sandy told him that Elspeth needed help, he had volunteered his time. He seemed like a nice boy, and Sandy was counting on his assistance. She really didn't want to be the one to shatter his illusion of a romantic relationship with Elspeth.

Hopefully he won't bring it up.

'So,' began Gordon, 'Are you, uh, Elspeth's flatmate?'

Here we go.

'Yeah. We're old friends.'

'Okay,' he grunted.

Change the subject.

'We almost there?'

Another car passed, splashing rivers of light across the road. Other vehicles were few and far between now. Ever since the turnoff, Sandy could count the number of cars they had seen on one hand. The last real sign of civilisation had been a McDonald's service station. She made a mental note to stop there on the way back and grab something to eat. Her stomach grumbled in response.

'Think so,' Gordon replied. 'I've never been. I only know the address because I'm part of the group e-mail. Does she, uh, ever mention me? Elspeth, I mean?'

'Sure, but only when she's praying to your shrine. So why weren't you on location?'

'My what? Oh, right. Uh, I'm just the editor. Robert says I don't have to be on set.' He paused. 'Also, he hates me and wishes I was dead.'

Sandy laughed. 'I've heard that, yeah. He thinks you fucked up his last movie.'

Gordon took his eyes from the road for a moment. 'She told you that?'

'Yeah.'

He smiled. 'Cool.'

'So did you?'

'Did I what?'

'Fuck up his last movie?'

It was Gordon's turn to laugh. 'No. It was all messed up to begin with. *Burns Night*, jeez. You ever see it? I don't remember you being at the screening.'

'She asked me not to go, but I snuck in and watched from the back. I was wearing a disguise and everything.' She laughed at the memory, of the comically oversized shades and hat she had worn, and then thought of Elspeth being coerced by Robert into stripping off for this new movie, and balled her hands into fists. That bastard...

'Should be a road leading off to the right soon,' said Gordon. 'Keep your eyes peeled.'

Sandy watched as the wall of pine trees whizzed past, the moon reflecting off the wet tarmac. She saw a flash of red within the forest, clothes or a bag or something, but thought nothing of it.

'Scary out there, huh?'

Gordon nodded. 'Kinda glad I'm not alone.' He looked at Sandy. 'Hey, um, don't tell Elspeth I said that.'

'Our little secret,' smiled Sandy. Suddenly she pointed. 'There, look!'

Gordon slammed the brakes, the car skidding, then regained control before they jackknifed off the road. Here, the trees parted, allowing access to a dirt track that snaked its way through the gap, before being swallowed by the darkness of the midnight forest.

'Is that it?' she asked. Gordon manoeuvred the car across

the road and came to a stop on the other side, facing down the track, switching on his full beams.

He shrugged. 'I mean…I guess there's only one way to find out. Do you see a sign or anything?'

'Nope. But look, there're tyre tracks in the mud.'

'Any of them Elspeth's?'

Sandy stared at him. 'How the fuck should I know?'

'Yeah, sorry. That was dumb.'

'Don't worry,' smiled Sandy. 'I won't tell Elspeth.'

'You're her girlfriend, aren't you?'

Sandy considered her response. No harm in telling him, she supposed. Here he was, driving her around in the middle of the night. He deserved to know the truth.

'Yup.'

'You could have told me.'

She touched his arm. 'I'm sorry. It's just, we like our privacy.'

'I knew it,' he said after a while. 'And then when I got your message…'

Sandy nodded again. She wasn't sure what to say, and wished they could get going again.

'I've heard rumours, but I never thought they were true. She doesn't, y'know…'

'What? Look like a lesbian?'

Gordon chuckled. 'Yeah, I think that's what I was going to say. Sorry.'

'That's okay. We don't all wear dungarees and have crew cuts, Gordon. It's 2019.'

'I know, I know. I'm sorry.' He failed to mask the hurt in his voice, and it irritated Sandy.

'She really does like you. As a friend.'

Gordon smiled at her. 'I'm such an idiot.'

'You are. Now, how about we get moving? I'd rather not spend the rest of the night in the middle of nowhere.'

'Good idea.' Gordon started the car, the lights flooding back on. He pressed his foot to the accelerator and the vehicle gasped forward then stopped, the wheels spinning uselessly in the mud.

'Shit.'

'What's wrong? Are we stuck?'

Gordon let the engine die and turned to Sandy.

'Did you bring a jacket?'

Sandy leaned against the headrest and closed her eyes.

This was going to be the longest night of her life.

19

IT WAS AFTER MIDNIGHT WHEN THE SHOWER SCENE ROLLED around.

The house was as cold as a morgue, the wind rattling the window frames, central heating a luxury that Mr Crawford had never bothered to install. The tiled floor was freezing beneath Elspeth's bare feet as she huddled in a dressing gown while the crew set up, her head throbbing.

'Are we recording sound?' she asked anyone who was listening. She hoped not. Then at least Deek could wait outside. One less pair of eyes caressing her body.

'Yup,' said Robert. He framed the shot using his hands in that clichéd way all directors do in publicity stills. He looked frustrated and sat next to her.

'How are you doing?' he asked in a soft voice, the one he had used with Hannah at the start of the shoot. Without waiting for an answer, he continued. 'You're doing a great job, you know that? You're a terrific actress. Believable, sexy, vulnerable. I'm glad I lost Hannah. You're ten times the actress she could ever be.' He smiled at her and placed his hand on hers. 'I'm really proud of you.'

Elspeth smiled back and said, 'I'm not getting my tits out for you, Robert.'

He pulled his hand away. 'Fuck, Elspeth. The scene won't work without it. We can't get the framing right.'

'You are so predictable. Drop the nice guy act, Robert. I've known you long enough.'

'Fine. Then you also know how much this means to me. How much this means to all of us.'

Here we go again, thought Elspeth.

'Come on, Els,' said Laura. 'Just from behind. You've got a cute wee bum, nothing to be ashamed of.'

'Damn right,' sniggered Aiden.

Robert glared at him and changed tactic. 'You kind of owe us one.'

'I don't owe you shit, any of you. This is my fucking body we're talking about.'

'And our careers,' said Laura. Somehow it was worse coming from her. Elspeth felt tears sting her eyes, and she blinked them away.

'I can't.'

'Why not?' said Aiden. 'I'd do it, I don't care.'

'It's different.'

'It's not,' agreed Laura. 'Look, there'd be no closeups or anything.'

'Yeah, I've heard that one before.'

'We wouldn't do that to you. You're our friend.'

Then the tears did come, hot and salty. It was Laura who came to her rescue. 'Right guys, everyone out. I need to talk to Elspeth alone, girl to girl.'

Grudgingly, the boys left the room, milling around outside like maggots festering in an open wound. Laura placed an arm around Elspeth, holding her close.

'Hey, come on, it's okay. Don't cry.'

'I don't want to do it,' said Elspeth, her face buried in Laura's shoulder.

'Why not?'

'I don't know. It's embarrassing, everyone looking at me.'

'I know. But you have to do it.'

Elspeth pulled back. 'What did you say?'

Laura smiled thinly. 'I said, you have to do it. You don't have a fucking choice Elspeth, and you know it, deep down you know it. You've always been the weak link, riding our coattails. Set designer, what a waste of time. What good have you done on this shoot so far apart from flirting with the lead actress?'

'I—I haven't done that.'

'So then you admit you've done nothing?'

Elspeth's mind raced out of control. Had she been flirting? Was it that obvious? Laura continued.

'You piss and moan about everything, you don't help with the equipment, you undermine Robert at every turn.'

Elspeth stared at her, her eyes wide and wet. 'That's not true. None of that's true.'

'It's true, Elspeth. And we *all* know it. We talk about it when you're not around. Everyone does. Everyone in uni thinks you're a fraud, even the tutors. So why don't you stop thinking about yourself for once in your life and help us out?' She laughed bitterly. 'You realise this is all your own doing, don't you? You told Hannah to leave, we all know it. The guilt is all over your face. You probably did it so she would fuck you. Well, even Hannah could spot a loser from a mile off. Don't blame us for making you do this. It's all your fault, a result of your bad decisions. You are responsible for everything, Elspeth. But you've fucked us over for the last time.'

She leaned in close enough for Elspeth to smell her lip balm.

'So stop *fucking* around and do the scene the way it was written, and remember that you've no one to blame but yourself.' Laura wiped a tear from Elspeth's cheek. 'Do we understand each other?'

Elspeth swallowed hard and nodded. Her mind reeled in confusion and anger.

'Great,' said Laura. 'Now sort your face out and I'll be in with the boys in two minutes.' She smiled, then walked to the door, before turning back to Elspeth. 'I'm glad we could come to an agreement.'

With that, she left the room.

Elspeth sucked in deep breaths, the oxygen helping to calm her nerves. Her hands were shaking. She looked at her reflection and saw the face of a fraud. Was it true? Did everyone say that behind her back? Were they laughing at her, her tutors humouring her until graduation day, when she would get on stage to receive her award and everyone would laugh at her until she ran crying from the building?

She looked at herself through swollen, puffy eyes and splashed cold water on her face.

A fraud. It was true. After her speech to Hannah this morning, how the tables had turned. If Hannah could see her now, about to let her *own* body be exploited.

The door opened and Robert, Deek and Aiden entered, Laura coming in last, unable to wipe the self-satisfied little smirk from her face.

'Are we ready?' Robert asked.

Without thinking, Elspeth nodded.

You can't do this. It's wrong. Everything is wrong.

Too late. She had agreed to it now. She deserved this.

Run. Run to your car and get the hell out of Dodge.

But it was her fault. She knew it was. Laura had told her.

Robert placed his hands on Elspeth's shoulders. 'Thank you,' he said. 'I truly appreciate this. You'll be fine, I promise.' He lifted her face up to his. 'Can I get a smile?'

Elspeth forced a grimace. 'Just from behind?' she said, her voice a shadow in the darkness.

'That's all, Elspeth. That's all we need. I'd never ask you to do anything you're not comfortable with.' He looked her up and down. 'You look beautiful, honestly. You should have been an actress.' He withdrew, a snake-charmer without a flute, the insincerity dripping from him like a leaky tap.

Elspeth splashed her face again, hardly recognising the girl in the mirror that stared back at her through haunted, wounded eyes.

'Okay Els,' said Robert (she wished everyone would stop calling her that), 'You know the scene. Are you ready?'

She nodded. It was all she could do right now. Words didn't carry enough power.

'Sound rolling?'

'Rolling.'

'Camera rolling?'

'Rolling.'

Laura stepped in front of the camera with the clapperboard. *Her* clapperboard. It seemed an absurd thing to get worked up about, but that was Elspeth's job. That's what *she* should be doing right now.

'Scene six, shot one, take one.' She slammed the board shut and Elspeth jumped.

'And...*action*.'

Elspeth stared, blinded by the lights. It took her a moment to remember what was happening, what she was doing here.

'Action,' said Robert again, more insistently. Elspeth

picked up the brush and ran it through her hair. 'That's good,' said Robert. 'You're angry. You're upset. Show us.'

Deek held the boom mic towards Elspeth. If he had actually been recording sound, he would have been furious at Robert talking all through the take. They both knew he wasn't. They all knew, except Elspeth.

'Okay, stand up.'

She stood up.

'Now face the camera.'

She faced the camera.

'You know what to do now.'

She knew.

It was like an out-of-body experience. She could see herself from their point of view, alone and afraid. Unsteady hands reached for her top button. Were they hers? Yes, those were her hands, working of their own accord. They had to be. Why else would they be doing what they were doing?

One button. Two buttons. Three. Four.

She closed her eyes and thought of Sandy. She would be home, waiting for Elspeth to climb into bed with more horror stories from the front-lines of student filmmaking. She pictured Sandy's kind face, her blonde hair, her soft, plump lips.

This is for you, Sandy, thought Elspeth. *It's just you and me here. Just you and me, no one else. No one watching but you, and that's okay because I love you and I trust you and I know you'd never let anything bad happen to me.*

She ran out of buttons, the blouse hanging open. The red of her bra stood out like blood on snow. The blouse fell to the floor, to

the floor of our bedroom, as you smile at me and I know that everything's okay, it's just another day, another evening together.

'Perfect,' said Robert. 'You're doing great.'

She felt their eyes on her, watching as she tried to control her breathing, slow it down. Her hands fell to her jeans, to undo the button, but they were numb, useless.

It's okay, said Sandy. *We're alone. Come to bed, lie here with me. Take your jeans off, leave them on the floor. I'm cold, and you're always so warm! Quick, get into bed and give me a hug.*

She worked the button loose, then felt for the zipper. It came down so easily. The waves crashed outside, rain hammering the window, but all she could hear was a buzzing white noise and the sledgehammer blows of her heart in her ears, too fast, too fast by far. She lowered her jeans, down past her thighs, then further, to her knees, her ankles, and then she stepped out of them.

Just from behind, that was the agreement. She turned away from them.

'Cut!' yelled Robert, jolting her back to reality. 'Jesus Christ, Elspeth, what the fuck?'

20

ELSPETH WHIRLED TO FACE THEM, ASHEN-FACED, HER THROAT like sandpaper.

'What's wrong?' she said.

'What's wrong? What's wrong? Take a look at yourself. What are you fucking wearing?'

'I...I...'

Aiden laughed.

'Jesus Christ,' said Laura. 'Batman? How old are you?'

Elspeth caught herself in the mirror. She turned from it, looking back over her shoulder. There, on the seat of her underpants, was the classic yellow and black bat-symbol.

'What?' she said, utterly disorientated. 'I like Batman.' She shook her head. How was she in a position where she had to explain her choice of underwear to a group of arseholes?

'She likes Batman,' said Aiden, dissolving into giggles. 'I bet Deek has a pair of those!'

'Shut it, I do not!'

Robert put his head in his hands as Elspeth tried to process what was happening.

'Elspeth, my dear,' he said in his most condescending tone, 'This scene is supposed to be...erotic. And here you are, in the middle of this sensual moment, parading your arse around in Batman knickers. I mean, do you want everyone to laugh at you?'

Her hands tightened into balls. It helped to snap her out of her fear-induced lethargy. 'You know, Robert, I didn't really expect anyone to *see* my underwear today. I'm sorry they're not *erotic* enough for you, you talentless fucking cunt.'

That shut them up for a minute.

She took the time to grab her clothes, throwing her jeans back on. She wanted to storm out, but there was nowhere to go, the four of them effectively blocking the only exit. Elspeth supposed that was no accident.

'Okay, I'm sorry, Els,' he said. 'I am. I just didn't expect that from a grown woman.'

'If you're trying to apologise, you're making a real shitty job of it,' she snapped, slipping back into the blouse and pulling it tight across her chest.

'No, honestly, I truly am sorry. Can we go again? Please?'

Elspeth went to the sink and took a drink of water. 'And what about Batman?' she asked sarcastically.

She looked at Robert, saw the wheels turning, imagined a hamster on a running wheel inside his head, powering up his synapses. He turned to Laura.

'What are you wearing?'

'Excuse me?'

'Under there,' he said, gesturing at her dress. 'What are you wearing?'

Elspeth watched Aiden and Deek, two naughty little schoolboys giggling about girls' underpants. She had never been so disgusted.

'I'm not wearing any,' said Laura, trying to kill the subject stone dead.

'Bollocks,' said Robert. 'You never go commando. Come on, let's see them.'

'But...'

'Hurry up. Deek, Aiden, look away. That's my woman I'm talking to.'

Oh yes, heaven forbid that those two jerks should see his woman in her underwear. After all, she's his own private property.

Laura lifted her dress. Robert nodded.

'Red. Perfect. They'll match her bra. Take them off.'

Silence.

'You bastard,' said Laura. 'You rotten, filthy bastard.'

She reached under the hem of her dress and stepped out of her underwear, throwing them at Robert. He, in turn, handed them to Elspeth.

'Put these on,' he said. When he turned back to Laura, she struck him across the face.

'Go to hell,' she said, pushing Deek aside, kicking the door open and slamming it shut behind her.

'Laura,' he shouted after her. 'Fuck!'

Elspeth placed the underwear next to the sink and smiled. Robert glared at her. 'I'm not through with you yet, Elspeth. But right now, take ten. I need a fucking smoke.'

He stormed out of the bathroom, his face clouded with anger.

And then there were three.

'I'm gonna get the 50mm lens,' lied Aiden.

That left two of them.

Deek looked at Elspeth.

Elspeth looked at Deek.

'That went well,' she said.

And then she laughed.

21

LAURA ENTERED THE ACTORS' ROOM. SHE GLIMPSED HER FACE in the mirror, her cheeks so red they were turning purple.

'Bastard. That fucking bastard.'

She paced the floor, working off the excess energy. How could he humiliate her like that? His own girlfriend!

It was one thing to shame Elspeth. Laura had never liked her, never liked the way Robert had looked at her. She enjoyed watching Elspeth suffer. About time that bitch was taken down a peg or two. But for Robert to turn on her, in front of the crew, in front of Deek and Aiden...

In front of *Elspeth*.

It was too far.

'Well, fuck you and your stupid movie, Robert. We're done.'

She lay on the bed. She was so tired. Tired of uni, tired of Robert and his twisted games.

She despised him, and yet she loved him. The problem was, he knew it. She supposed he wasn't that bad, not really. There were much worse men out there. Okay, so she hated the way his roving eyes always seemed to be looking at other women, but he had never acted on it. How many women could say the same about *their* boyfriend?

He was an artist, and artists are temperamental. It's a fact, and everyone knows it. If they tell you otherwise, they're lying.

She was being overdramatic. Yes, that was it. She needed to cool down. Take a breath. One thing she could not do, however, was return to the set in a dress *sans* underwear. She walked over to the costume box and looked for an outfit to change into. Then she spotted Elspeth's jeans neatly folded on the chair. Ideal. They were a similar size. It was only fair. If Elspeth was going to wear her underwear, she would wear her jeans.

She thought she heard something, a noise from the walls, but ignored it, unaware she was being watched.

Robert stomped down the stairs and across the landing.

He was losing them, the film slipping through his fingers like fine grains of sand in an hourglass counting down the seconds of his faltering career.

Everything was going wrong. He had no control anymore. His crew were rebelling. It was an uprising. A mutiny! He figured he still had Deek and Aiden on his side, but he needed Laura. If she didn't have another talk with Elspeth, he knew she would walk. He cursed himself for his outburst. Idiot! He should have just left it alone.

He reached the front door and turned the handle. Nothing happened.

Because Laura has the keys.

'Fuck. Shit, fuck, *fuck*.'

He couldn't even have a smoke! Oh well, Mr Crawford wasn't around, and by the time he got home, they would be long gone. Robert shoved a Marlboro in his mouth and lit it. It did the trick. He inhaled, blowing the smoke out through his nostrils.

Could he convince Elspeth to shoot the scene again?

Maybe he didn't have to. They had plenty of footage of Hannah in the shower, most of which didn't feature her face thanks to Aiden's overzealous zooming. They could cut around it, have Elspeth get undressed, then cut to Hannah in the nude. Everyone would assume it was Elspeth. He laughed to himself. He couldn't wait to tell Laura. Surely that would help clear the air between them?

He just had to keep Elspeth out of the editing suite, and hope that she didn't kill him when she saw the final version.

A shadow at the far end of the hall caught his eye.

'Laura? That you?' he shouted.

There was no reply.

He finished his cigarette, crushed the butt into a potted plant and lit another.

Aiden couldn't believe his luck. This was the greatest day of his entire fuckin' life. The greatest.

First Hannah. Then Elspeth.

Now he crept between the walls, squinting at Laura through the peephole. His producer. Robert's girlfriend. Owner of the finest titties he'd ever seen.

His cock stiffened. Damn, he needed more space, but beggars can't be choosers. Opportunities like these come along once in a lifetime.

He had followed her on the off-chance she might bitch

about Robert. That would have been funny, but she had already gotten it out of her system by the time he had wriggled his way through the cramped crawlspace.

Aiden had not expected her to take her dress off.

He rubbed his cock as she stood there, practically naked, his eyes travelling up her body. He was going to come. Nothing would stop him this time. This was the only chance he would ever have to see Laura naked, or near-enough. He was glad he had waited. If Robert knew what he was up to...

He pushed the thought of Robert aside, nearing release. He had to hurry, Laura was getting dressed too quickly.

Aiden took one last look at Laura, and then everything went to hell.

The jeans were cold on Laura's legs as she hauled them up. The fit wasn't bad, looser around her butt than she was used to, but without any underwear, that might prove to be a good thing. Now all she needed was a top.

Elspeth's white vest was on the chair, but Laura wanted something warmer. This damn house was freezing. She rifled through the costume bag and selected a navy blue knitted Shetland jumper, ideal for cold weather.

The door opened. Had she forgotten to lock it?

'Hey, I'm getting dressed in here!' shouted Laura, holding the jumper across her chest.

'*What the fuck!*' gasped a muffled voice from behind her. It sounded like Aiden. She turned and faced the wall, searching for him, unable to comprehend how he had gotten into the room.

Then she felt the hand on her shoulder. It wasn't

Robert's. His hands were soft, the benefit of never indulging in manual labour.

No, this hand was rough, almost wooden. It stank too, of sex. Blood and sex. It squeezed too hard, the nails — they felt more like claws — digging in below her collarbone.

'Oh god, stop it, who is this?' she growled, lashing out backwards, her fist striking someone, something, bouncing off it like a wasp hitting a window, and then her arm was caught, grabbed by the thing and twisted up behind her back, higher and higher until something snapped.

'Laura!' shouted Aiden, blinking through the peephole at the atrocity taking place mere feet in front of him.

But she couldn't answer, couldn't speak, couldn't even scream. The pain was too much to bear, her arm broken at the elbow, the thing's claws digging into the tender flesh above her breast until they penetrated the skin, rending and tearing. She felt warm blood spilling out of her chest, splashing on the floor, coming up her throat. The thing forced its filthy, stinking fingers all the way in, curling them around her collarbone until it had a firm grip, then lifted her off the ground as if carrying a suitcase, flinging her across the room where she smacked into the wall right in front of Aiden's peephole.

She slid down, leaving a smeared red trail on the floral wallpaper, and tried desperately to crawl away, every part of her burning in agony.

She didn't get far.

It towered over her, reaching down and grabbing her by the clavicle again, hauling Laura to her feet. It tightened its grip on the bone, digging its putrid fingers into the meat of her shoulder, putting its other hand on the top of her dizzy, nauseous head and pulling, pulling hard until her collarbone snapped and was wrenched from her body. She sank to the floor, briefly thankful for the darkness that swooned over her eyes.

She couldn't see the creature raise her own splintered bone in its ghastly, foul hands and bring it rushing down towards her heart.

22

ELSPETH AND DEEK SAT IN SILENCE FOR SEVERAL MINUTES.

Deek's eyes kept darting back to Laura's bunched up underpants on the counter by the sink. Elspeth picked them up and tossed them into his lap.

'There you are, Deek. Take a good look. Keep 'em, in fact.'

He stared at the red briefs, daring himself to pick them up, to run his fingers over the lace. He did. They were so soft, so delicate. He threw them back at Elspeth, his cheeks flushed with colour.

'Robert told you to put them on,' he spluttered. 'Want me to wait outside?'

She smiled. 'That won't be happening.'

'What d'ya mean? You don't want to piss off Robert.'

'It's over. I'm through with it. Robert's just lost his second actress of the day,' she said, putting *actress* in air quotes.

'You cannae. What'll we do?'

'I dunno.' She picked up Laura's underwear again and threw them, hitting Deek in the face. 'Why don't *you* put them on and do the scene? Might be your big break.'

'So what, we all fail then? Four years of uni down the drain because you're too shy?'

Elspeth looked out the window, at the water dribbling down the pane. The sea outside was rough, white waves sweeping across the ocean like wild horses. In the distance, she saw the lights of a freighter ship making its treacherous journey.

'It's nothing to do with being shy. Or being prissy, or being a virgin, or whatever excuse your feeble brain comes up with next. It's about being used, abused and exploited.'

'But you agreed to it, in Maccie Dees.'

'Coerced, maybe. Bullied, definitely. There was four of you, ganging up on me. I felt like I didn't have a choice, but you know what? I did. I *do*. It just took me a while to clear my head and realise that.'

'I never bullied you,' he said, sounding like a petulant child. 'It was all Robert and Laura.'

She turned from the window and looked him square in the eyes.

'But you did nothing to stop them.'

'So go then,' he said, unable to hold her gaze. 'Fuck off. Why are you even still here?'

She thought about it for a while before answering.

'Because I want to see Robert's face when I tell him. I want him to understand that he can't treat women — or anyone — like shit he scrapes off his shoe. And, I want to tell him what a pathetic, half-arsed fucking hack he is.'

'You're a cold wee bitch.'

That made Elspeth smile even wider. 'You have to be, Deek. You have to be to survive.'

He shook his head. He didn't understand.

How could he?

Survival was something Aiden knew very little about. The closest he had ever come to death was a car crash at 3am on a deserted city street in Glasgow. The driver had been reckless. The driver had been intoxicated.

The driver had been Aiden, and the car had been stolen.

Driving sixty in a thirty zone, he had careened into a parked car. Luckily, he had suffered only minor injuries; whiplash, and a nasty bruise on his chest from the steering wheel. Jenny Douglas, his then-girlfriend, had not been so fortunate. Her crumpled body lying across the bonnet was the reason Aiden would never forget to wear a seatbelt until the day he died. If he closed his eyes, he could still see the shards of broken windshield embedded in her face, one protruding from her eye socket, reaching out to him with her dying breaths, weeping tears of blood.

He got off with it. Money really can buy you anything, and while Aiden and his father rarely spoke, his dad was always willing to splash the cash if it meant keeping his son out of trouble. As a prominent local Conservative politician, it was more for his benefit than Aiden's, but Aiden couldn't complain.

He hadn't even been punished. For a while, the thought of Jenny gurgling at him as she died was punishment enough. Then, when he found out she had been carrying his baby, he decided it was more of a reprieve. He was far too young for that bullshit.

Now he faced death again for the first time since that night, and his reaction was much the same; shrill, high-pitched screams of terror. The expression on Laura's face reminded him of Jenny in her death-throes, a look of wretched, agonised horror and confusion. The big man brought the bone down towards her and Aiden leaned his head away from the peephole.

Her assailant was huge, and appeared to be naked. Unable to see his face, Aiden assumed it was Mr Crawford. They were of a similar height, though he didn't remember Crawford being built like a brick shit-house, and couldn't imagine him acting with such unrestrained animal ferocity.

He heard the bone entering Laura's body. What a dreadful sound it was, nothing like in the movies. He realised how trivial onscreen deaths were. They never got it right, couldn't replicate the true gut-churning horror of real life.

Aiden vividly recalled working with Deek to create foley sound effects for the murder scenes of *Burns Night*. For bones breaking, they had snapped carrots and celery. For the stabbings, they had hacked at an apple, and for the beheading, they chopped a lettuce in two. They had thought it was all so convincing, so *real*.

Now the artifice was revealed, the curtain pulled aside. Death was always more shocking and also, somehow, more *pitiful* in real life. The way the human body was exposed as a useless sack of meat, the way people reacted not with stoicism and bravery, but with the dread realisation that their life was over.

Unlike in the movies, Laura never even screamed. She gurgled, spat, bled and begged, but she never raised her voice, as if she knew it wouldn't make a difference. When death descends, screaming about it ain't gonna help.

Yeah, try telling yourself that.

Aiden worked to get himself under control. The walls were closing in on him. He stopped screaming, sucking in great deep breaths, his belly pressing against the wooden panels.

He remained like that, gasping in lungfuls of air, until he noticed the new silence. Laura was dead, he knew that. He didn't have to look, but he also knew he had to. Ignoring his now-limp penis, he sidestepped towards the peephole.

Where he came face-to-face with the man.

That is, if you could call it a face.

Aiden had no time to brood on the matter.

The man raised a solid steel fire poker and rammed it into the wall. Unable to react, Aiden closed his eyes and awaited the inevitable. The metal tip smashed through the wood two inches to the side of his head, stabbing fiercely into the brick behind him. Aiden yelped and recoiled as the implement withdrew, shambling his way to the left, moving sideways through the crawlspace. The poker rammed through the wall again, this time in the direction he was heading. Light from the bedroom streamed in through the two new openings like bullet-holes in a cartoon. Aiden wanted to drop to his knees, but there was no room, barely even enough space to stand in the claustrophobic passage. The poker entered the crawlspace again, but it was getting further away.

He's lost me, thought Aiden.

Then the wood splintered, and the poker plunged into his stomach, just above the navel. His body shuddered, his bladder letting itself go, warmth spreading around his crotch and running down his legs.

The poker twisted as it was removed and he felt his guts churn. He was dimly aware of fists pounding on a door, anxious shouts, people calling his name. He wanted to reply. In fact, he had never wanted anything more in his entire life.

'That dick of yours is gonna get you in a lot of trouble one day,' his ex-girlfriend Rosie had once said to him. How right she was. He was going to die because of Laura's muff.

What a way to go, huh?

The poker thrust through once more, lower this time. It pierced Aiden's dick, pulling it back beneath his legs. The tip would have pinned it to the wall, but the member wasn't long enough to reach. Instead it split right up the middle, peeling apart like a banana skin.

The knocking on the door became louder, more frenzied, until it was drowned out by an acute wailing sound. It was coming from his own mouth.

The man extracted the poker again, taking the last shreds of Aiden's manhood with it.

It was all too much for him.

Aiden died with the ruin of his penis dangling between his legs.

23

Elspeth and Deek hammered their fists against the locked door.

'Laura? Aiden?' they shouted, unable to figure out which of the pair was in the room and screaming bloody murder. It sounded like a girl, or a boy soprano.

'Open the door!'

Footsteps stomped down the hallway and Elspeth spun. Robert came dashing towards them, his lit cigarette leaving a thin trail of smoke behind him.

'What's going on?'

'We heard screaming,' said Elspeth. 'In here, but it's locked.'

Robert's face darkened. 'Laura,' was all he said. He pushed Elspeth to one side and grabbed Deek, who nodded. No words were necessary. The two of them stepped back before charging forwards, their shoulders impacting on the solid oak door. It made no difference.

They tried again, but it was like running at a brick wall. Deek rubbed his shoulder. Their only hope was that the lock was old, rusted and breakable. Together they barrelled into the door again, and this time it gave slightly.

'Wait,' said Elspeth. They looked at her expectantly, taking deep breaths. 'It's gone quiet.'

Somehow, that was worse.

'Come on,' grunted Robert. They powered on, striking the wood. Something splintered on the other side. Exhausted, the two boys stopped. Robert ushered Deek out of the way and aimed a fierce kick at the handle.

The door smashed open, the remains of the lock crashing to the floor with a metallic thud, loose screws rolling across the floorboards.

Elspeth entered first, Robert's bravado momentarily deserting him. Her hands felt empty and she longed for some kind of weapon.

The room looked normal apart from several holes in the wall, a dark reddish-brown liquid leaking from them. From one of them protruded a long, metal fireplace poker.

'Oh shit,' said Robert, entering at a safe distance behind Elspeth. 'Is that...'

'Blood,' Her voice was distant. She walked towards the wall, then stepped in something and slipped, her feet skidding out from under her, landing flat on her back. It should have been hilarious, but no one laughed.

Not when they saw what she had slid on.

A large pool of fresh blood, some of it already disappearing through the cracks in the floorboards. Elspeth scrambled to her feet, eyes searching the room for the body, for the source of this atrocity.

'Is this a joke?' said Deek, his voice cracking mid-sentence.

Robert shrank back against the wall. 'Laura?'

Elspeth walked towards the poker. She grasped it, the

handle slippery with gore. The blood was still warm, and she choked back the urge to vomit. She turned to face the others.

'There's something behind this wall.'

Robert stared at her, horrified. With one sharp movement Elspeth yanked the poker free, a small gout of blood dribbling down the ugly wallpaper.

Kneeling, Elspeth peered through one of the holes. 'I can't see, it's too dark.' She turned to Robert. 'We have to break it down.'

Robert shook his head, unable to stop doing so. 'I can't.'

Elspeth gingerly cradled the poker.

'It's okay. I'll do it.'

She felt the weight of the weapon in her hands. Weapon? Yes, she supposed that was right. Anything can be a weapon in the right hands.

Or the wrong ones.

She raised the poker above her head and brought it down hard against the wall. It reminded her of summers spent on her grandmother's croft in the Scottish Highlands, chopping firewood with an axe and collecting eggs from the chicken coop. It was a nice memory, one tinged with an aching nostalgia. She cast the thought aside, unwilling to taint it.

The plaster cracked and fell to the ground, exposing the thin wood beneath. She hacked away, the poker ricocheting off the wall with a clang, until sweat dripped down her forehead and her hands ached from the sharp vibrations.

Soon, she had created a small hole, just big enough to poke her head through. Behind it she saw the familiar red brick exterior, only this time from the inside. It made her feel like a prisoner trying to escape from jail, only to be thwarted by another wall. She dropped the poker and looked back at Robert and Deek.

'Guess we'd better see what's there,' she said, hoping one of the boys would volunteer.

When neither did, she balanced on her tiptoes and peered into the gap. A cool draft hurtled through the crawl-space, which was twelve inches at the most. A tight squeeze.

The void stank like the toilets in a student flat, a potent cocktail of shit, piss and cum. She turned her head and there was Aiden, his face a grisly mask of horror. His jaw hung open, and she saw he had bitten off the tip of his tongue. His eyes had rolled back into his head leaving just the bloodshot whites, like a man who's seen the face of the devil.

She stepped away, nearly collapsing onto the bed. Thank god it was there, or else she'd be flat on her arse again.

'What did you see? Was it her?'

Elspeth shook her head, her whole body numb. 'Aiden. He's dead.'

'Bullshit,' said Robert, running over to look himself. 'Oh god,' he cried, flattening himself against the wall for support. It was no use. He slid down, then leaned to the side and vomited.

'We need to call the police,' said Elspeth, her head woozy and confused. When no one answered, she repeated herself.

'We can't do that,' wheezed Robert, shuffling away from the small puddle of vomit.

'Why not?'

Robert wiped flecks of bile from his mouth. 'We're not supposed to be here.' A tear rolled down his cheek, disappearing into his matted beard. 'We broke in.'

'What did this, what the fuck did this,' said Deek.

Elspeth ignored him, preferring to dwell on practicalities, anything to keep her mind from wandering down dark corridors and through doors better left unopened.

'So what? Aiden's dead, and Laura could be—'

'We don't know that. We don't know shit right now. She could be anywhere. We've not checked the house. She could be downstairs having a glass of wine.'

'That's *blood*, Robert, and it belonged to someone. We need to call the police.'

'I don't want to go to jail,' whimpered Deek.

'There's no way to phone from here,' said Robert in a dazed torpor. 'No signal.'

'Then we'll use your uncle's phone.'

'He doesn't have one.'

'Okay. Then we get in our cars and drive until we find a signal.'

'The Maccie Dee's had a phone,' said Deek.

'Yeah. Yeah, it did.' She turned towards the broken door. 'Come on, let's get out of here.'

'Uh, guys,' said Robert. 'It's not as simple as that.'

'And why not?'

'I, uh, didn't want anyone to leave. So I locked the front door.'

'So unlock it,' snapped Elspeth. She had no time for this. Aiden was dead, and Laura was missing. Come to think of it, where was Ted?

'That's the problem,' said Robert. 'I gave Laura the keys.'

Elspeth took a moment to process this new information. A queasy mixture of fear and anger rose in the pit of her stomach.

'You what?'

'She was keeping them safe. In case you tried to run,

Elspeth.' She listened, disregarding the implication that it was all her fault.

'We could break the door down.'

'That door?' said Robert. 'No chance. It's a fucking beast.'

'So what are we gonna do?' sobbed Deek.

'Her clothes,' said Elspeth. 'My god, her clothes!' She jogged over to the bed and lifted Laura's black-and-white striped dress. She turned the dress this way and that, searching for pockets.

There were none.

'Fuck's sake! Why can't they just give women fucking pockets!' She hurled the useless garment across the room, where it fluttered to the floor like a dying bird.

'Now what?' asked Robert.

'We have to find her. Dead or alive, she must still have the key on her.'

'She's *alive*,' said Robert.

Elspeth nodded. 'I know. I'm sorry. But we really have to get out of here. Because whatever did *that* to Aiden...'

Is still in the house. Here. With us.

She couldn't bring herself to say it out loud, and she didn't have to. Just by looking at Robert's ghostly white face she knew he understood.

She turned her attention to the pool of blood. A trail of it led away, suggesting a body had been dragged to the wardrobe, the door of which hung half-open invitingly.

A creeping unease brushed her spine. It had to be a joke. A weird, sick joke.

'In there,' she said, pointing. 'There's someone in *there*.'

'What the fuck is going on,' said Deek, his face drained of blood. He ran his hand over his shaved head, the rasping noise of the small bristles setting Elspeth's teeth on edge.

'We need to look,' she said.

'Be my fucking guest,' said Robert.

'It could be Laura in there, you know.'

'Could be a lot of things in there.'

Fuck it.

Elspeth advanced on the wardrobe. The trail of gore was thick. Someone had lost a *lot* of blood.

Someone was probably dead.

Laura.

'Hurry up,' said Robert.

'Fuck off,' she replied, not looking back. She was only a few feet away now. What if something was lurking in there, ready to strike? A killer? A monster?

Don't be ridiculous, there's no such thing as monsters.

She held the poker out, her arm at full stretch, and nudged the door with the tip. It shivered open.

Dresses. Masses of them, filling the interior of the wardrobe. On the right was the champagne-coloured gown that Hannah had worn for the flashback, hanging in a see-through garment bag like a corpse in a slaughterhouse.

Shut up.

The trail led further inside. How deep did this wardrobe go? All the way to Narnia?

'What's happening?' asked Robert, lurking far behind her.

Elspeth ground her teeth together. No matter what the circumstances, somehow Robert always managed to piss her off. In a way, she was glad of the brief distraction, something to take her mind off the irregular beating of her own heart, or the dread that nipped at her heels.

'My battery's dead,' she said. 'How about you guys?'

'We don't have any signal.'

'I know. Just need someone to shine a light in here.'

Deek pulled out his phone and handed it to Robert, who handed it to Elspeth. 'You're so interested, you shine it.'

'Coward,' she muttered, swiping up on the iPhone and switching on the torch. The beam illuminated the floor of the wardrobe, beneath the hanging vintage dresses and robes and gowns. More blood, but no body.

'There's nothing in here.'

'That's not possible.'

Elspeth heard the agony in Robert's voice. 'We don't know it's Laura,' she said, as if that were some sort of reassurance.

She scooched down on her hands and knees, squinting into the black of the wardrobe, where the shadows met the backboard. She crawled in further, the trail ending. It vanished into the wall as if...

'Wait a minute.'

'What is it?'

She flattened her palms against the light wooden panelling.

'What are you doing?' asked Robert. Elspeth carried on. If she could just find...

Click

...the switch.

The back of the wardrobe creaked open.

'Guys,' said Elspeth softly, taking a deep breath. 'You'd better come see this.'

24

SANDY CLAMPED HER JAW SHUT TO STOP HER TEETH FROM chattering.

Gordon's jacket was wrapped around her shoulders, the light from their phones guiding them to apparent safety. On either side the trees swayed like boats at sea, tumbling and rolling in the gale, while far above them, faded stars gasped their dying breaths.

'At least the rain's off,' said Gordon.

'Don't jinx it,' snapped Sandy, trying not to sound as angry and frustrated as she felt, her feet sinking into the ravenous mud.

'I'm sorry,' he repeated, apologising for the thousandth time.

'Just keep walking. We can't be far now.'

Gordon squinted at his phone and pointed. 'According to the map, we could cut through the woods. It's a straight line to the Manor that way.'

They both followed his finger into the black woodland chasm.

The situation was dire, but it was not yet desperate enough to face the sinister mysteries of the forest.

And so on they trailed, the two weary travellers, through mud and wind and darkness, in search of the elusive Crawford Manor. To no one's surprise, the rain started to fall again.

When your luck's out, it's really out.

Something in the trees wailed, or roared, or screamed.

'We must be close,' said Gordon, shivering through his light fleecy top as the drizzle soaked into his skin, his hands pale and pruned like he'd just crawled out of the sea.

Sandy was beginning to question whether this had been a good idea. What if Elspeth was fine, and filming was continuing as normal, and she had misunderstood the context of the message, a breakdown in communication?

It had happened before, and would happen again, the unfailingly fallible means of modern technology no match for basic human interaction.

Another roar from the forest. It was getting louder, *closer*, a metallic shriek, and then she turned, blinded by lights that penetrated the darkness, her own torchlight fading into insignificance. She froze, her hand shooting uselessly to her eyes.

'My god,' she said, and Gordon felt it too. Fear, *real* fear, the primal kind that mankind often erroneously believes it has left behind.

The headlights dimmed, the Land Rover stopping mere feet from where they stood. Sandy noticed Gordon had taken her hand, but she didn't pull away.

The door opened and someone got out.

'What on God's green Earth are you two doing out here in this weather?' asked Ross Crawford, adopting a note of sympathy in his voice, something he had gotten very good at over the years. The dishevelled pair stared at him as if at a ghost. He didn't wait for a response. 'Here, get in, you'll catch your bloody death in this!'

'Oh god, thank you,' rattled Sandy, her teeth chattering from nerves or cold or both, as she slopped her way through the mud towards the vehicle, Gordon trailing close behind.

Inside, the heating was on, and the sodden pair marinaded in the back seats. The car smelt faintly of mud and copper.

'Thank you, Mister...' Sandy trailed off, giving their rescuer a chance to introduce himself and receive her profuse thanks.

'Aye, it's a hell of a night to be out,' he said instead. 'Where, might I ask, are you headed?' He adjusted the rearview mirror for a better look. 'Don't get a lot of visitors out this way.'

They sat, the engine purring. Gordon spoke, his voice shockingly childlike.

'We're on our way to see a friend.'

'Oh,' nodded the man. 'And where might she be?'

'Crawford Manor,' said Sandy. 'Do you know it?'

'Aye, I know it. No one there now though, unless you're looking for phantoms.' He laughed mirthlessly, dry bones rattling in a coffin.

Gordon stole a nervous glance at Sandy. 'No, they're shooting a film there. Overnight. But we think our friend is in trouble, so we were on our way to pick her up when my car got stuck. I guess you saw it back there?'

'Aye, I did. Damn near crashed into it.'

'I'm sorry,' said Gordon, but Crawford spoke over him.

'Dangerous road, that. Comes out of nowhere. Overnight, you said?'

A moment's silence, until Sandy realised he had asked them a question.

'That's right.' More silence. She tried to fill it. 'A night shoot.'

'A night shoot, eh?' He rolled the words around his mouth.

'That's right.'

The man sighed heavily, his windscreen wipers sweeping monotonously back and forth, back and forth, doing little to stem the tide. 'There were certainly some youths there earlier, but I saw them vacate the premises.'

Sandy and Gordon shared a glance as the car idled in the storm.

'So you've seen them?' she asked. 'We're looking for Elspeth. Um, perhaps you know her? Brown hair, about five-eight, very pretty.'

'Beautiful,' interjected Gordon.

'Elizabeth?' said Crawford in a faraway voice.

'No, sir. Elspeth. She was part of the crew.'

'Oh, I used to know an Elizabeth. I'll be damned, did I ever know an Elizabeth. After all, she was my wife.' His hands slipped from the steering wheel and rested in his lap. He sounded like he was smiling. 'You are, however, correct in your assessment. She was our Lord's most beautiful creation, an angel sent from heaven. When I met her that day, at Bobby Forrester's birthday party, I couldn't take my eyes off her. None of us could.'

'Excuse me sir, if you—'

'We went on a few dates. Oh, not like the kind you young folk go on now, with your drink and your drugs. Courting, that's what Elizabeth called it. She wanted to be courted, and I was a willing suitor. Walks in the park, hand in hand, a stolen kiss here, a brief embrace there.'

'That's a nice story. I wonder, could—'

'We married young. Life was a whirlwind back then, not a care in the world. Some say youth is wasted on the young, but not on Elizabeth. So free, so impulsive, so alive.' He turned to face them.

'She's dead now.'

Sandy didn't know what to say. 'I'm...I'm sorry to hear that.'

'Oh, Elizabeth. The things they did to you. Those awful, terrible things. Heaven lost a special angel that day.'

'Again, I'm sorry to hear that,' said Sandy, trying to remain patient. This man was doing *them* a favour. So what if he was wants to get misty-eyed and reminisce for a minute?

He paused, his gaze meeting Sandy's in the rear-view mirror. She looked away.

'Here son, sit up front with me, if you wouldn't mind. My eyes don't do so well at night. In the darkness.'

Sandy squeezed Gordon's arm. He nodded at her, and mouthed, 'It's okay.'

'Come on, son. It's getting late. Let's find your friends, shall we? Crawford Manor is just a short drive down the road.'

'Just coming, sir.'

Sandy held onto his arm, her heart pounding.

'Don't,' she whispered.

He smiled back, and opened the car door, the wind howling through the vehicle, rain soaking the already drenched leather seats. It slammed shut behind him, leaving Sandy and Crawford alone in the car for what felt like an eternity.

Sandy noticed the old man's rheumy eyes watching her

in the mirror. She scratched self-consciously at her cheek and checked the time. Nearly one.

I'm coming, Ellie. Don't do anything silly.

The door flew open and she came close to screaming as Gordon threw himself into the passenger seat.

'Aye,' said Crawford, 'It's not a night to be out and about. Not tonight, not a night like this.'

'Can you drop us near Crawford Manor, please?' asked Sandy. 'If it's not too much trouble, I mean.'

'Aye, not many visitors out here, I tell you. Not these days. Back when Elizabeth, God rest her soul, was still with us, then maybe, aye, maybe. Back then, folk would call in every now and again. Well-wishers, do-gooders. Even the minister, on occasion.' He chuckled. 'Oh, she would get herself in a right flap when he called round. Here son, be a good lad and hand me that bag at your feet.'

Gordon did as asked, lifting the surprisingly heavy holdall and passing it to the old man.

'Sir, we appreciate your assistance, but we really have to get a move on,' said Sandy.

'They stopped coming around the time we had our first child.'

Sandy clenched her fists. How many steps down memory lane was he going to take tonight, here in this car, in the middle of the woods, in the pouring rain?

'Sir, could we—'

'Aye, after Sebastian, they stopped coming. Who can blame them? He was a funny lad, always out-of-sorts. A real temper.' The man craned his neck around to look at Sandy and twitched out a wink. 'A real eye for the ladies too.'

'Right, that's it,' said Sandy, reaching for the door handle. She pulled it and nothing happened.

The old man opened his black bag. He nodded to himself.

'Such a temper. I don't know where he got it from.'

Sandy tugged the handle again.

'Excuse me, could you let me out please? I seem to be stuck, and quite frankly, you're creeping me the fuck out.'

'Sandy!' gasped Gordon. 'Look mister, I'm sorry, but—'

Crawford unsheathed the aged butcher knife from his bag and held it for a second, allowing Gordon just enough time to see it, to understand, to register the fact that he was about to die, before thrusting it into his stomach, the blade slicing through his thin fleece and even thinner skin, the sharpness in his belly alarming Gordon almost as much as the sensation of the blood leaving his body.

Sandy screamed and threw herself back against the seat as Crawford twisted the blade and hot blood gurgled from the wound, Gordon shaking, starting to spasm. He turned to Sandy, eyes wide but already glazing over.

She shook the doorhandle, pulled at it, forced it. She turned her head away, pointed her elbow, and rammed it at the window. The glass splintered but did not break.

If only it had.

25

ELSPETH SHONE THE TORCHLIGHT AS FAR AS IT WOULD GO, BUT the beam was hopelessly insignificant. She followed the trail of blood across the threadbare carpet until it disappeared from view, as Robert and Deek crowded into the wardrobe alongside her.

'Holy shit,' said Robert.

'You think it's Mr Crawford?' asked Deek.

'His car's not there,' said Elspeth absently, her mind sorting through possibilities.

Robert turned to Elspeth. 'If anything's happened to her, it's your fault.'

She stared back at him, dumbfounded. 'What?'

'This is all your fault. If Laura is hurt or...worse, then I'm gonna kill you.'

Elspeth swallowed. It sounded so loud. '*My* fault?'

'You heard.'

'Listen Robert, this is not the time. Once we're out of this, I will happily tell you precisely how and why this whole thing is *your* fucking fault. But right now, we've got more important things to deal with, okay?'

'I'm just saying, Elspeth. I'll kill you.'

'Calm down, man,' said Deek.

'Don't tell me to calm down ya wee wanker.'

Elspeth sighed. 'This is getting us nowhere. Come on, I'm going in.' With that, she parted the dresses and crawled through, the blood soaking through the knees of her jeans. She clambered out into the darkness and stood, directing the beam around the room.

It was a child's bedroom, but one forever trapped in the mists of time. Her torch picked out a wooden cot-bed, blankets draped over the edges, near-cocooned in cobwebs. Faded paintings hung crooked from the walls. The blood trail snaked its way across the carpet, past an old-fashioned rocking horse that lay on its side, then round a corner and out of sight. She saw a dolls' house, hand-carved to resemble Crawford Manor. Next to it sat a wind-up monkey, the kind that crashed cymbals together and gave generations of children nightmares.

'Elspeth,' whispered Robert from the other side of the wall. 'Is it safe?'

She crouched. 'I think so. It's an old bedroom.' Somehow she kept her voice under control. In the back of her mind, there remained the possibility that this was an elaborate prank, one they were all in on, a way to get back at her for some perceived slight or misdemeanour. The idea grew more absurd by the second, but until she found hard evidence, she would cling to it for dear life.

Oh yeah? Aiden's corpse not real enough for you?

Robert wriggled through after her, Deek behind him. Elspeth shone the light over to where the door should be. It had been bricked up. She searched for a light switch and found nothing, then cast the beam over the ceiling.

No light.

Makes sense. No light, no need for a light switch.

Nine alphabet blocks were laid out across a solitary shelf, arranged in such a way as to spell out a name.

'Sebastian,' said Elspeth, not realising she was speaking out loud.

'Follow the blood.' She turned to Robert, shining the light in his eyes. He winced. In the glare he looked like a heavily bearded ghost. She trained the beam back on the carpet, finding the crimson trail.

Why, oh why did it have to go round a corner?

This damned house, with its hidden rooms and secret passageways. Why couldn't they have filmed the movie in Robert's flat, or in the university library, or in a fucking park or something?

'Come on,' urged Robert, noticeably not volunteering to take the torch and go first.

She inched forwards, one step at a time. Robert had shown them some films before the commencement of shooting, to give them an idea of what he was aiming for with the visual style and tone of *The Haunting of Lacey Carmichael.*

The Beyond. Suspiria. The House With Laughing Windows. A bunch more she couldn't remember the names of. Most had been enjoyable in their own way, but she had always been frustrated by the pacing. The characters did everything so slowly! Particularly *The Beyond*, where everyone seemed to be shot in slow motion. And yet here she was, shuffling her way along as if she was blindfolded. Her foot kicked a ragged, moth-eaten teddy bear, and it rolled onto its side, the black eyes regarding her coldly, its stitched smile a twisted mockery of innocence.

The trail veered past a window, and Elspeth opened the

curtains, letting the thin veil of moonlight into the dank, musty room. Out there even the seagulls were quiet, the rain turning to a fine misty drizzle.

She turned the corner and faced a narrow passageway, following the blood, the trail growing thinner until it came to a stop, ending in a punctuation mark of dark red. A single pool in the middle of the carpet, on one side a rack filled with black, buckled shoes, and on the other a little velvet suit suspended from a rail. Elspeth moved aside to let the others see.

'It just stops,' said Robert.

'Is there another passageway?' asked Deek.

A phantom breath swept up Elspeth's spine, and her stomach sank.

Drip. Drip.

She didn't want to look up, she really didn't.

Drip. Drip.

Someone had to do it. Either the boys hadn't noticed, or they were pretending not to. The torch was cold in her hands.

Deek's torch, she reminded herself.

Drip. Drip.

What was that film they had watched...the one where the tap kept dripping, and the woman was haunted by an old lady with a ghoulish face who floated across—

Oh stop it! That's not helping.

She raised the torch, prepared for the iPhone battery to die. It didn't.

'Oh, come on,' she said. 'You've got to be fucking kidding me.'

Over their heads swayed a frayed white rope, a ceramic duck on the end. Elspeth's eyes travelled up the cord, to the old wooden trapdoor above them, from which came the relentless *drip drip* of blood, the beads splashing into the pool below.

Whatever they were looking for, it was up there now.

Up in the attic.

26

'Ladies first,' whispered Robert.

'Now you're a fucking gentleman, aye?'

Elspeth reached for the cord, placing one hand on her wrist to keep it steady. Her fingers brushed the ceramic duck, its blank white eyes reminding her of Aiden. Poor Aiden, crushed behind a wall, dead. Her classmate. She had considered him a friend once. She supposed in time she would learn to forget recent history and remember him for his good points, maybe even make up a few. That's the rule when someone dies, a tacit understanding between mourners to forget the bad shit and rake around in their subconscious for good memories. You can be an asshole all your life, but chances are you'll die a saint.

'Elspeth?'

'Yeah, okay, I'm getting there.'

Why don't one of you two fuckers do it?

She had seen enough horror films to know what might come next. If a character opens a trapdoor, there's a seventy-five percent chance a body will fall out. She tugged on the cord once and the hatch shuddered open a crack.

Damn it. It's not locked.

'You checked the room thoroughly, yeah? The keys were definitely not there?'

'Nope,' said Robert. 'Laura has them.'

'Okay.' She pulled the cord again and stepped back as the trapdoor creaked fully open and a rickety wooden ladder unfurled, coming to rest on two shallow indentions on the carpet.

The flow of blood briefly intensified, some of it splattering onto Elspeth's shoulder.

'Oh Laura,' said Robert. Elspeth angled the torch into the void. The light caught the beams in the ceiling and nothing else, her shaking hand causing the shadows to jitter restlessly.

'I can't do it.'

Although unable to see their faces, Elspeth knew they were both looking at her.

'You have to,' said Robert, though he didn't elaborate on why that was the case.

'No, I'm through being pushed around. I'm not going.'

'Fine. Give Deek the torch.'

'Aw naw man, fuck that for a laugh. What if someone's up there?'

'Then be quick.'

'She's your girlfriend, like. You go.'

Stalemate. Elspeth saw the frightened faces of the boys, pale and glassy-eyed. Is that what she looked like?

'Scissor-paper-stone?' said Deek. Robert took an eternity to respond.

'Aye, I s'pose so.' He held up his fist. 'Best of three?'

Deek nodded. Elspeth wanted to laugh at the absurdity. A children's game to decide which of them should go into the attic and grab the keys from the corpse of their friend. It was too ridiculous for words. And yet, she had no better ideas.

'On three,' said Robert.

They pumped their fists three times and revealed.

Robert scissors, Deek paper.

First blood to Robert.

'Come on,' said Elspeth. For all they knew, Laura was still alive up there. Well...

They went again.

This time, Robert was scissors and Deek was rock.

One apiece. It would all come down to the third and final battle. There could only be one victor, and more importantly, one loser.

They faced each other, both trying not to cry, to hide their fear. As men, they had grown up being taught that emotions were for the weak. Instead, they looked up to a masculine ideal of strength and courage. For Deek, it was playing rugby on the weekends. For Robert, it was the power he exerted over the women on his film sets. None of it was any use now. No amount of bravado or dick pics could help out here.

One, two, three, draw!

Scissors for Robert again, three times in a row. Typical of Robert and his mind games. But Deek had beaten him at his own game, his fist clenched. Rock beats scissors. He had won. He looked his friend in the eyes.

It was the hollowest of victories.

Robert bit his lip, his trembling fist still raised. He tried to smile. 'Best of five?'

'I'm sorry, man,' was all Deek could say. He leaned against the ladder and wiped tears from his eyes. 'I'm so sorry.'

He was still apologising when something reached down and grabbed him under the chin.

He tried to shout, but the enormous hands were pulling him up so fast he couldn't open his mouth, the rungs of the ladder smacking into his back, his feet kicking frantically. Elspeth leapt forwards, latching onto Deek's right leg.

'Help!' she shouted. Robert hesitated, and for a second she thought the rat-bastard was going to run. Then he joined her, just in time. Her own feet were leaving the carpet as she clung onto Deek with grim determination. Robert tried to grab Deek's other leg, but it was like catching a trout as it swims upstream.

Elspeth was several inches off the ground and she trapped her own foot under a rung to halt her ascent.

'Deek!' she shouted fruitlessly, as if doing so would miraculously bring him back down the ladder. Specks of blood dotted her face.

Robert had a hold of one leg now, and between them they managed to tug Deek back. Then a jet of blood hit Elspeth, getting in her eyes, her mouth. Deek kicked out violently, breaking free as Elspeth fell to the floor, the carpet doing little to cushion her fall. She got back up. He was almost out of reach now, plasma brimming over the side of the vent. She jumped for his leg, bashing her thigh off the ladder, her fingers stretching for his foot, the hem of his jeans, anything.

There was a roar from the attic. Colossal. Inhuman. It reverberated throughout the manor, deep and guttural.

'Oh fuck this,' said Robert. He let go of Deek's leg just as Elspeth caught the other.

'Robert!' she shouted, but he didn't look back. He vanished round the corner, back into the darkness of the room. Without Robert, the fight was over. Deek's legs shot up into the air, disappearing from sight. Elspeth rested her face against the ladder, realising for the first time that she was crying.

It was so dark that Deek wasn't sure if his eyes were open or closed. He weighed fourteen stone, and yet the man in the attic lifted him like a rag doll, almost wrenching his jaw out of its socket. Deek felt the pressure abate as he was hurled through the air, until he hit the wall and then, with depressing inevitability, the floor. Suddenly the room was bright, a blinding white light dancing across his eyes.

My head. I hit my fucking head.

A hand closed around his mouth. It stank of shit and piss and blood, the ragged nails digging into his cheeks and gouging out thin strips of flesh, his feet lifting as the thing carried him by the jaw. He slammed against the wall, his head ricocheting off the brick, his mind clouding. He dropped to his feet but his legs were useless jelly and he sank to the floor.

'Please,' he sobbed, 'Leave me alone. I want my mum.'

Fingers invaded his mouth, both hands, hooking onto the sides and pulling it apart into a rictus grin. Deek clamped his own stubby hands over the wrists. They were huge, brute-like, a caveman's hands.

They pulled his mouth wider, Deek's cheeks and lips burning from the pressure. He clawed at the hands, though he may as well have scratched at stone as he plummeted down a mountainside. He bit down on the fingers, his canine teeth digging into the filthy flesh, piercing the skin and drawing blood. It did no good.

He heard his cheeks tear before he felt it, his upper lip

splitting and ripping up to his nostrils, the loose skin peeling back, exposing gums and rows of stained red teeth. His mouth filled with blood and it poured down his chin as the hands invaded further into his face, dragging the skin apart until it burst and the lower half of his face came away, the sagging flesh of his own lips and jaw and chin held aloft by some monster.

As he lost consciousness, he thought he heard the thing chewing.

The cold embrace of death enveloped him, and he welcomed it with open arms.

27

ROBERT RAN, TRIPPING OVER THE ROCKING HORSE BUT maintaining his balance. The moonlight streamed through the window, enough for him to identify the hole in the wall, the one that led back to safety. He fell to his knees and threw himself into it, the vintage dresses brushing his hair as he emerged from the darkness into the reassuring comfort of the bedroom, with its lights and doors and exits.

Nothing seemed real anymore, the room an illusion. It felt too safe. The house was trying to deceive him, trick him into believing he had escaped. He glanced back as he headed towards the door. No Elspeth, nor anything chasing him.

He wondered if Elspeth was dead too. She wouldn't last five minutes against the maddening strength of whoever was in that attic.

There had to be a way out, a set of windows with no bars on them, or a side door he could break through. He thought of Laura and more tears came. And Deek. Poor Deek.

It should have been me.

He could worry about that later.

He raced down the hallway and hit the stairs running, gripping the rail. This was not the time to lose his footing and break an ankle.

Or his neck.

The door seemed ridiculously far away, down an endless corridor. He thought of the scene from *Poltergeist* where the hallway keeps stretching as JoBeth Williams runs down it, but this wasn't one of his movies.

This was real.

Before he knew it, he smacked hard into the front door. He rattled the handle, pulled on it, shoulder-barged it, but the imposing doorway didn't so much as budge.

That was okay. That was fine.

Because now the handle was turning all by itself.

Elspeth willed her body to move.

Part of her — a strange, hidden part of her — wanted to go up there and help Deek.

Well, *try* to help him.

The other part — the rational, sensible part — knew he was already dead, like Aiden and probably Laura.

Dead.

Now we'll never *finish the film.*

She almost laughed. Was she losing her mind? And if so, who could blame her? Robert had run. Why hadn't she? Why couldn't she tear her eyes away from that trapdoor? Deek's iPhone lay face down on the carpet, the torchlight perfectly framing the wooden hatch. Feet stomped upstairs. A bang. She backed away.

The phone.

She scooped it up.

It was time to leave.

The darkness opened up before her, a black hole of despair, as she followed the lonely beam. The low entrance to the room was set into a stone Victorian fireplace. She hadn't noticed that before. Why would she? Something clicked in her mind, deep in her subconscious, but she couldn't dwell on it, didn't have time. She crawled through the fireplace, scraping her arm against the sides hard enough to leave a gash, and emerged in the actors' room, the blood on the ground still as wet as morning dew. Elspeth got to her feet, leapt over the crimson puddle and headed for the door. She nudged it open and slipped out into the hallway.

The lights were on, the tungsten filaments swaying hypnotically in crystal strands that dangled from chandeliers. Her heart thudding, Elspeth dropped to her knees and pushed her body up against the bannister, listening, but all she could hear were the waves beating against the rock way down below, crash, withdraw, crash, withdraw. She crept along, towards the strange old staircase with the stuffed bear beneath it, towards the only way out of this place. And now, *yes*, she heard banging, meaty fists pounding solid oak.

Robert.

Peering through the rail she saw him, his back to her, facing down the massive door. She wanted to cry out but some primal sixth sense, a long-dormant animal instinct, made her stop.

Instead she watched as the door opened from the outside.

≈

Robert took one step backwards, allowing the door to tremble open, his body tensing, poised to run, awaiting a starter's pistol that would never be fired. He sidled through the gap then stopped, his exit blocked.

'Uncle?' he tried to say, but Crawford was too quick for him.

Robert's last thought was, *for an old man, he sure is fast.*

Crawford's hand came up like a jack-in-the-box, and Robert braced himself for the impact of a hard uppercut. He never saw the knife, barely even felt it, as it thrust through his jaw and punctured his tongue. He tried to pull away, but was snagged on the blade. Crawford let go and Robert tottered backwards, grasping weakly at the knife handle, his soft, rich-kid fingers brushing against it.

He collapsed, his skull cracking as it hit the wooden floor. He clutched the hilt of the knife and wrenched it out, a torrent of blood gushing forth. Crawford came to him, pressing his knee down hard onto Robert's chest. The boy waved the knife around feebly, grazing Crawford's hand as the older man plucked it from his grasp.

'Please,' gasped Robert with his dying breaths, blood jetting down his shirt. 'Please...'

Crawford placed the knife to one side, then raised his fist and punched Robert in the face, again and again and again, until he no longer recognised the bloody pulp as his own relative. Then he picked up the knife and slammed it into Robert's stomach, drawing the blade up, slicing through the pliant flesh until once again, all was still.

Crawford's posture changed. He slumped forward and sighed.

He shook his head.

He punched the wall so hard it dislodged some plaster.

'Why?' he shouted, his voice straining. 'Why didn't you leave? I told you all to leave. I watched you do it, I watched you go. Why did you come back?'

From her vantage point by the stairs, Elspeth waited, unmoving, afraid to make a sound, afraid to breathe. It was Robert's uncle! He had killed Aiden and Laura!

Wait, no, that wasn't possible. He had been outside.

So what? He *knew*.

He knew there was a killer in the house, a maniac, a psychopath. That was why he had wanted them out before dark.

To...to protect them?

'Is anyone still alive?' shouted Crawford. Elspeth didn't move. Robert's foot tapped out a rhythm on the floor as his body entered its death throes.

As if we're gonna answer, thought Elspeth. Then she remembered she was the last one left, unless Ted was hiding somewhere. It was possible. She stretched her legs to avoid cramp. Sitting still was hard work.

The door banged shut again.

She had to look. She had to act.

She had to do *something*.

Elspeth peeked round the corner of the stairs.

Crawford was gone, and Robert's body lay twitching on the floor, the convulsions slowing. The front door swung open. Crawford? Or the wind?

Fuck it.

Elspeth slithered down the steps as fast as she could, and when her feet touched the rug she quickstepped forwards on tip-toes like a frightened ballerina, nearing escape, closing in on the door. She had one chance.

She had to take it.

Twenty feet away, then fifteen, now ten. Her pace quickened. She felt the breeze on her face, the air cool and inviting. She stepped over Robert's corpse, smelt the foul odour of expelled bowels, and headed for the door.

It was almost within reach when something grabbed her ankle.

28

Elspeth crashed to the ground, landing awkwardly on her shoulder. She turned to see Robert, his fist gripped tightly around her ankle, looking at her through milky eyes, blood spilling from the sides of his mouth, his lips opening and closing.

He was still alive, but for how long? Could she help him? Where was Crawford, and was he coming back?

'Get off,' she spat, wriggling free, tears stinging her eyes. She put her hands on his, unwrapping his claw-like fingers.

She heard a car door slam.

Crawford.

'Robert, please,' she cried, but he didn't release. She wasn't even sure he could hear her.

Something outside, dragged across gravel.

She hooked her fingers between Robert's and lifted them, her knuckles whitening.

Footsteps, coming up the porch stairs.

She snapped one of Robert's fingers, then another. The pain didn't register on his face. 'I'm sorry,' she said, as the digits broke in her hands, *snap*, and then she was free. In a frenzy, she eyeballed the nearest door and hurled herself into the darkness, rolling behind a couch, breathless and horrified.

The front door swung open and Crawford lumbered in, his heavy work boots stomping on the floor. He looked down at Robert, the young director grasping his crooked fingers at thin air. Crawford's face wrinkled in distaste. He positioned his boot over Robert's head and stomped, the skull splintering, crushed underfoot. Robert died instantly, tiny porcelain shards of bone visible amongst the ripe fruit of his brain matter.

Elspeth watched from inside the room, her eyes glazing over. She felt sick, her stomach lurching violently, and yet she couldn't look away. The front door — her only escape route — slammed shut. The key turned in the lock, the bolt grinding into place.

I'm going to die here.

Crawford walked into view again, dragging something. A black bin bag. He hauled it down the corridor somewhere. When he came back, he repeated the action with two more bags. Finally, he heaved Robert's limp carcass down the hallway and out of Elspeth's line of vision.

He'll come for me next. Him and that thing in the attic. They'll find me and kill me like the others.

The footsteps returned. Elspeth scurried into the corner of the room, out of sight. The door unlocked again and Crawford spoke, his voice no longer the deep baritone it had once been.

'I'm sorry,' he said. 'I don't know if anyone's alive in here, but if you are, please know, I'm truly sorry. I never meant for this to happen. I never wanted this life, never asked for it. I wouldn't have wished it on the devil himself. But it ends here. It ends now.' He paused, then screamed, 'What'll you do now, eh? I'm leaving! Who's going to feed you *now*?'

The door closed and Elspeth was alone.

Well...not quite.

29

Ross Crawford, who had lived in Crawford manor for every one of his seventy-four years, shed no tears as he trudged down the stairs like a condemned man. He had seen too much.

Done too much.

Too much harm, too much...evil. Yes, that was it. Evil. It was his responsibility, and he accepted the blame. But he had done it for his children. Seven of them, each more...*abnormal* than the last.

A God-fearing man all his life, he often wondered why the saviour had chosen to smite him. His poor, forsaken wife had gone mad, her brain rotting from the inside. It was the manor's fault.

It got into your head.

Still, he had tended to her, and made sure the children were always in bed while she was up. It would do her no good to see them. Then one evening, he arrived home late. Just once, that was all it took. He raced home, cutting through the woods, barging through the house until he found her, his beloved Elizabeth, in the kitchen.

He was too late.

The children had already eaten.

Elizabeth, her clothes and flesh torn, lying on her back, the ungodly brood crowded around her, their hands slick with blood, mouths full of stringy intestines.

And there on top of her, licking a handful of meat, had been Sebastian. The children dispersed, leaving Crawford alone with his wife's remains. He cradled her severed head for a while, gently weeping, and then phoned his younger brother Arthur.

Only someone without children could have done what they did that evening.

Arthur Crawford — who years later would father a son of his own, Robert — arrived in the early hours of the morning. Without a word, Ross Crawford handed his brother a hunting rifle, and together they stalked the halls of Crawford Manor.

One by one the children fell, six in all. By sunrise, only the eldest remained.

Sebastian.

Crawford sent Arthur home, unable to articulate his gratitude, then buried his offspring in an unmarked grave, and his wife (or what was left of her) in a small plot of land overlooking the sea, by the bench where Crawford had proposed to her all those years ago.

When he went back inside, Sebastian was waiting. Crawford aimed the rifle, his son's bizarre visage caught in the crosshairs, but he was unable to shoot. Sebastian was his firstborn. He couldn't let the Crawford legacy crumble to dust. He couldn't!

Instead, Crawford poured himself a brandy and fell asleep in his chair. He awoke to the sound of a baby crying, a gurgling, mewling shriek that was barely human. He did the maths, remembered the faces of his children as he and Arthur had murdered them. Six. He had buried six bodies. There couldn't be more. It wasn't possible.

It wasn't *possible*.

Then Sebastian entered, carrying something in his arms. He handed the skinless bundle to Crawford, who ran one hand over the glistening, sinewy cheek. The baby quietened, gazing up at her grandfather for the first time...

Life went on. Crawford performed his fatherly (and grandfatherly) duties to the best of his limited ability. He fed his new children, and clothed them too, until no clothes would fit. He tried to make suits from old curtains, but Elizabeth had been the seamstress of the family.

He even installed the bars on the windows to stop them escaping, but after a while their apparent wanderlust trickled to nothing. They preferred the shadows, and the company of the rats and insects, avoiding daylight like hulking vampires, their eyes growing weaker, atrophying in the perpetual gloom of the manor. They stuck to the attic, using the crawlspaces to move around the house. Crawford rarely saw them. It was for the best. Their misshapen limbs and ghastly faces haunted his every waking moment, reflected back at him in the leafless branches of the trees, and the clarion call of the beasts in the woods.

He couldn't do it anymore. Let them starve. Let them die.

Let Sebastian rot in the dank pits of a thousand hells.

Now he clambered into the Land Rover and settled himself, sipping the last dregs from a bottle of brandy, before turfing the empty container out of the window. The engine sprang into life and he thought of the hundreds of bodies he had transported over the years, in the back of this very vehicle.

In the nineteen-seventies, it was easy. Hitch-hikers were

a common sight, and DNA was years away. After a while, he started to pick up prostitutes. On particularly lean days, he had cruised past school playgrounds in far-off cities with a bag of sweeties and a sharpened knife in the passenger seat.

The children were the easiest, but provided the least satisfying meal. Sebastian preferred the women. Yes, he had always been a *real* ladies' man.

'I accept my fate in the eyes of the Almighty,' Crawford whispered, taking one look back at Crawford Manor, charnel house of atrocities for five decades. He saw a young woman staring at him through the window. One of the film crew. My God, she was still alive!

Ross Crawford smiled and waved at Elspeth, then pressed his foot to the accelerator. The car shot forwards, tearing up grass and mud, onwards, onwards, and then over the edge of the cliff.

As the waves and the rocks rushed up to greet him, Crawford closed his eyes and awaited his judgement.

30

Elspeth watched as Crawford's car tipped over the edge of the cliff face and plummeted into darkness. Several seconds later a colossal bang rang out across the bay. She waited for an explosion of light to ripple over the sea, but none came, and just like that it was over, another black candle snuffed out.

You're on your own now.

Why? Why had he left her here? The question plagued her thoughts. She took her hands from the window, leaving ghostly impressions on the glass, and turned to the door, still ajar.

When is a door not a door? When it's ajar!

'Don't lose it, don't lose it,' she whispered.

Tonight, Robert Burns...in hell.

The raging cyclone of her mind tormented her. What was she doing here, trapped in this nightmare? She should be home in bed, snuggled up next to Sandy, fighting to keep her share of the covers from her restless lover.

'There has to be a way out. There has to be.'

What about the front door? It was as good a place as any. Perhaps Robert's uncle had forgotten to lock it when he left?

Yeah, sure.

Summoning up every last reserve of courage, Elspeth shuffled through the room, becoming intimately familiar with each creak and groan of the floorboards. Wooden flooring is like a ghost. It's not there during the day, but at night, after the witching hour, it comes out to play, each step wringing forth menacing grunts and wails.

She tried the front door with shaking, white hands.

Locked, obviously.

Then she remembered Deek's phone and took it from her pocket.

Dead.

Fucking iPhones, she thought, but now was not the time to lament the poor battery consumption of consumer gadgets. But wait! Maybe Robert had his? And maybe, just maybe, it still had some life in it. There had to be somewhere in this house where she could get a signal. Or what about Crawford? There had to be a phone in one of the rooms, though she couldn't recall seeing one.

Think, Elspeth, think!

She decided to try Robert. His body wouldn't be hard to locate. Just follow the trail of blood, like some X-rated Wizard of Oz.

And watch out for that thing in the attic.

She surprised herself by walking back down the hall, away from the exit, her breathing loud enough to be heard for miles around. Elspeth inched forwards, her eyes locked on the big stuffed bear, until she arrived at the corner. It was dark here, and she reached for the light switch, stopping herself just in time. In the blink of an eye, she had almost given away her location. Something thumped upstairs and she stopped for several minutes, holding her breath.

Satisfied no one was coming, she resumed her journey, finding her eyes had adjusted somewhat to the lack of light. The trail carried on down the corridor, then vanished beneath a door.

Well, what are you waiting for? Go on in.

Time was slow, meaningless. She could have stood there for ten minutes or ten hours, a statue made of flesh and bone. She didn't want to open the door, and yet she did, a hand — her own, surely — edging towards the handle, closing over the brass orb, tilting it one way — nothing — and then the other, the door opening, the hinges mercifully quiet.

Somehow she was inside, as if in a lucid dream, the door behind her shutting quietly. The light was already on, or had she switched it on herself? She couldn't say for sure. Everything was heightened, unreal.

Sheets of rain lashed the windows, running down the iron bars as she surveyed the room. An office. A desk, the top of which was empty of both paperwork and stationery. Bookshelves stretched to the ceiling, on which stood rows of dusty tomes on parenting, with some children's books thrown in for good measure.

Mrs Beeton's Book of Household Management.

The Cult of Childhood.

The Tiger Who Came to Tea.

But the trail of blood didn't stop in the office. It carried on, shimmering under the glare of the light, towards another door, one that Hannah had discovered only a few hours prior. Elspeth stared for a moment, struggling to comprehend the anachronism before her.

It was enormous, and made of metal, like a walk-in freezer.

This must be where he stores the bodies.

She didn't want to go in, but she had to.

Elspeth turned the handle and opened the door. There was nothing on earth that could have prepared her for what she would find behind it.

It was a slaughterhouse. Bodies — parts of them, at least — lying forgotten and discarded in the corners, frigid limbs jutting out obscenely, broken bones licked clean and deposited next to torn clothing and a glassy-eyed severed head that regarded her with horror. The teeth had been removed and pierced into the flesh; the cheeks, the nose, the eyes.

It was Ted.

'Oh god,' she whimpered, the room spinning, tilting, whirring. Robert lay face down in the centre alongside three black bin-liners, his head soggy and flattened. Elspeth took several deep breaths and staggered drunkenly inside, her hand clamped over her nostrils. She knelt by Robert's corpse. She had left him to die, even broken his fingers, and all to save herself.

It was him or both of you. And don't forget, he abandoned you first.

She checked his jacket pockets, patted down his jeans, pulled out a wallet and some keys, the dangling keychain bearing a photo of him and Laura at the funfair. There was everything except a phone.

Something thudded into Crawford's office, heavy and lumbering.

Elspeth looked around, her mind racing, but there was no way out.

She was trapped.

31

LEADEN STEPS, THE KIND THAT SET HEARTS RACING IN FEAR, clumped lethargically into the room. Elspeth scurried to the wall, to that rotten mass of limbs, ready to dive in, when a great shadow fell over her.

Sebastian was here.

She paused, frozen, and turned her head to look.

He stood tall, unnaturally tall, hunched over in the doorway. He was naked, his body covered in patches of mottled hair, his skin diabolically scarred, freshly picked scabs of raw flesh pockmarking his grotesque frame.

But it was his face. God, his face.

The features were twisted, the left side hanging in a permanent sneer, the bulbous lip dangling to below the nub of a chin. Deep grooves lined the eyes, one hidden by the tousled and filthy locks of his hair, matted red with crispy blood. He stared right at her, breathing, grunting, dribbles of saliva splattering the ground.

Elspeth wanted to scream, needed to, but her mouth would not cooperate, and so there she remained, a calf ready for the slaughter. She looked at him, eyes wide and staring and unbelieving.

She was going to die here.

Sebastian stared back, dropped clumsily to his knees, and crawled in, his hands outstretched, brushing the floor, searching. They found one of the black bags and he grabbed it and yanked it towards his hulking body like a sack of feathers, his strength inhuman.

Elspeth waited for him to pounce, to rend her limb from limb.

Sebastian clawed at the bag, shredding it, staring uselessly ahead, looking right at her.

He can't see me.

His fingers probed the bag, eyes fixed on the blank wall behind Elspeth.

He's blind.

She glanced towards the door. She was directly in Sebastian's line of sight, and yet he continued to paw at the black container, oblivious to her presence. He tore it open and Elspeth saw Gordon's face, his jaw slack and eyes white. She gasped, covering her mouth with her hand.

Sebastian stopped. He raised his head, tilted it towards her.

Elspeth held her breath. Could he hear her heart beating?

Sebastian sniffed, his nose twitching, air rasping through like a blocked drain. Elspeth didn't move.

The brute turned back to Gordon, running enormous, coarse hands over his face, caressing it, lifting it to his mouth. He took a bite out of Gordon's cheek. The sound was ghastly, a sheet of fabric torn from top to bottom, but chewy and crunchy and vile.

Fearful for her sanity, Elspeth closed her eyes.

Oh Gordon, dear Gordon, what are you doing here?

She sniffed back a tear. *He* would have stood up for her. Gordon would have had fought her corner. He was one of the good guys.

She felt air on her face, a rancid smell spiralling up her nostrils, coming in short, heavy bursts. She swallowed carefully and opened her eyes.

She was face to face with Sebastian.

He stared through her with blank, clouded eyes, licking his lips with a sandpaper tongue. A piece of raw meat dangled from his his teeth as he sniffed, inches from her face. Moving as gracefully as could be expected under the circumstances, Elspeth slid her body down, her legs gliding through the wet blood on the floor. Sebastian thrust his head forward to where Elspeth's had been mere seconds before. He ran his tongue over the wall as Elspeth slipped away soundlessly. She figured the dreadful stench of the room was confusing him. Anywhere else, and she'd probably be dead right now.

Or worse.

She slowly got to her feet and half-crawled, half-staggered out of the room, leaving the hideous man-thing to enjoy his savage feast, to chew on the flesh of her friend like it was a Sunday roast. Light-headed, Elspeth escaped from the office and back out into the hallway.

It was game over. No doubt about it. Without the key to the door, she—

The key! Laura has the key. Laura is in the attic. The beast is downstairs. This is it. This is your chance.

She had to get up to the attic while the beast was indisposed. She could find Laura, get the key and escape.

What else was she going to do? Sit here and die? Fight the giant hulking monster? She prowled down the hall, up the stairs, hardly thinking now, instinct taking over, the creaking of the floorboards beyond her control. She hoped the sound didn't travel. Soon, she found herself at the door to the actors' room, and then she was inside and standing by the wardrobe. She got down on her hands and knees, facing the darkness, this time with no torch to guide her. How much time did she have? Was Gordon a main course, or more of a snack?

Don't say that!

Without hesitation, she crawled through, the draught from above whispering through her hair. She thought of the fireplace she would emerge from, trying not to visualise that dreadful dark bedroom and the trapdoor to the attic. What awaited her at the top of that ladder? What fresh hell?

'Sebastian,' she said, dimly recalling the wooden blocks on the shelf. They had seemed so meaningless at the time, relics of a forgotten childhood. She groped blindly, an absurd parody of Sebastian, until her hand found the rungs of the ladder. They were wet and she knew why. It felt like hours since Deek had been hauled up through the trapdoor, but it was still dark outside. She couldn't wait for daylight. She had to find Laura, had to get that key while Sebastian was out of the picture.

Why was Gordon here? What mania had caused him to venture out on this night? Had Robert called him, asked him to come? She supposed they had needed all the help they could muster. Still, Robert must have been *desperate* to call on his own arch-nemesis.

And now they were both dead. What a waste. What a senseless, horrible waste.

Elspeth started to climb, taking each step slowly, left, right, left, right, mentally steeling herself, always listening, waiting for the dreadful clamour of Sebastian coming for her, biting and tearing.

Her head was level with the attic floor now, a shaft of weary moonlight penetrating the murky gloom through a small broken window, covered — like the rest of them — by iron bars that split the light asunder. The whole house was a prison in lockdown, and now the warden was dead and the inmates had taken over.

The smell in the attic was foul. As bad as the office? That was the smell of death. This was more like shit, and stale, musky sex.

Pick your poison.

The light drew Elspeth in and she climbed into the loft, her eyes adjusting, the floor wet with blood.

So much blood.

So many bodies.

They were piled high, carcasses in various stages of decomposition, stacked corpse upon corpse.

Elspeth scanned the floor. She thought she saw Deek, but the face was skinless, the clothes shredded. She kept looking. A white square in the corner of the attic caught her eye.

A mattress, with a body lying spreadeagled across it. It was female, and looked, for lack of a better term, somewhat *fresher* than the others. Elspeth shivered.

It was Laura.

She *had* to have the key on her, *had* to. Elspeth broke into a trot, no longer caring about the noise levels. Sebastian was far below her. She was safe here, for now at least.

Her foot snagged on something and she tripped,

sprawling face first onto the floor, her fingertips brushing the mattress, turning to see what had impeded her.

The shadows stirred.

Elspeth's heart sank.

Elliott was awake, and he wanted to play.

32

ELSPETH SHRANK BACK ACROSS THE GORE-DRENCHED FLOOR AS Sebastian's son Elliott shambled into consciousness, his twisted face contorting like melted clay. One eye sagged open, the withered orb drooping loose. He used a sharpened talon to pierce the eyeball, forcing it back into the socket and pulling his eyelid closed again, then lumbered towards the mattress, towards Elspeth. He had no lips, the skin rotted away, revealing tar-like gums.

His hands found Laura's bare feet. She was dead, her collarbone jutting from her breast.

Elspeth shuffled as far away as the claustrophobic interior would allow, bumping into a wall as Elliott crawled on top of Laura's corpse, his rancid penis stiffening as he ran his paws over her chest, his splintered nails leaving faint red lines on her skin. He wailed, a dreadful sound, an injured wolf, an abandoned infant, and Elspeth put her hands to her ears to block it out. He pressed his penis between Laura's legs and started to rut, his moan a horrid punctuation to his animal thrusts. Laura's body jerked back and forth, her expressionless face aimed at Elspeth.

The deranged brute sped up, pounding Laura with his necrophiliac urges and Elspeth knew she had to leave, had to get out now or this time she would surely lose her mind. There's only so much horror the human brain can handle.

And that's when she saw it, a moonlit sparkle between Laura's breasts.

The key.

Laura must have kept it in her bra, and Elliott's relentless assault was working it free. It lay there, half-in and half-out, a cruel trick of fate, fortune once again flipping Elspeth the bird.

She needed that key. It was her only chance.

The beast continued his unspeakable act, his vocalisations gaining in pitch. Elspeth slid along the floor on her stomach, the blood soaking through her blouse, until she reached the mattress, inches from Laura's cold, dead face.

The key had worked its way out as far as it would go, now snagged on the fabric of Laura's bra. Elspeth leaned over, her head directly above Laura's, eyes fixed on her only hope of escape. She stole a brief glance at the mutant, his face a tangle of depraved ecstasy, then inched an arm out over Laura's lurching body, her fingers reaching for the key, and she almost had it when Elliott came with a guttural scream, his eyes opening wide. He spasmed forwards, one deflated eyeball popping out from its socket and landing like a pickled onion in Elspeth's lap. She recoiled in revulsion, bile rising from her treacherous stomach as a wave of nausea washed over her.

The crude beast put his hands on Laura, searching for the misplaced organ, his nails cleaving ridges in her flesh and drawing blood. He came close to the key, Elspeth watching, rigid with fear. What if he found it? Would he know what it was?

'Mmmmmhhhhhmmm,' lamented Elliott. He balled his fists and smashed them into Laura's face. What if he alerted the other creature, that abomination? Elspeth pinched the soft orb between her fingers, lifting it from her lap and placing it delicately on Laura's prone torso.

He found it. His lipless mouth curled into something resembling pleasure as he plucked the eyeball from Laura and stuffed it into the waiting hollow. Elspeth took her chance. She grabbed the key with one hand, using the other for balance, and tugged. Elliott replaced his eyeball and swooned, falling forwards. Elspeth pulled hard, the lace tearing, the key coming loose as she snatched her hand back, the stocky beast collapsing forward, spent. His barrel-chest scraped her hand, the hairs like wire, as she clasped the key to her body like a talisman.

Elliott slumped over Laura, obscuring her with his considerable bulk. Elspeth shook her head, relief and horror grappling for supremacy. She turned and crawled towards the trapdoor. She was almost free.

Deep snores bounced throughout the attic as Elliott drifted off to sleep atop his prize. She waited, taking one last look around the third-floor abattoir. It was a horror-show. How many bodies? How long had this been going on?

Well, it stopped here. As her hands found the trapdoor she thought of the incredulous looks on the face of the police officers when she told them what she had found. They'd need some kind of SWAT team to storm the place. Or the military. She just hoped they'd believe her.

And that was when she noticed the quiet.

She squinted through the beam of moonlight, at the mattress, at Laura's body, uncovered and exposed.

Where was—

A hand grabbed at her hair from out of the shadows,

lifting Elspeth, her feet leaving the rungs of the ladder. She screamed, not caring who heard, lashing out. The pressure on her scalp was immense, and then she was flying, hurled through the air and landing jarringly on the attic floor. He came for her in a graceless trot, his whole body buckled and deformed, his hands out, reaching, always reaching. Elspeth looked around for a weapon. She found a bone and wielded it like a baseball bat, getting unsteadily to her feet. She swung as Elliott neared her, the bone striking him harmlessly on the arm. He lunged and she ducked, skittering to the side, a heap of decaying bodies breaking her fall. Thinking fast, she darted to the broken window and wrenched a shard of glass from the frame, slicing her hand. Elliott approached and Elspeth launched a pre-emptive strike, dashing towards him, rushing the sharpened fragment towards his face.

It struck home, piercing his cheek and gashing it open. He yelled something indecipherable and swung a heavy fist, catching Elspeth on the bridge of the nose. She fell hard, blood spilling from both nostrils, clutching onto the piece of glass with grim determination. He towered over her, a shambling man-thing, his tongue poking out from that blood-smeared cleft of a mouth. Elspeth gripped the glass, cutting deep canyons into her palms, and stabbed him in the thigh. Elliott roared. Elspeth whirled to his side, stabbing down, planting the fragment of glass into the back of Elliott's ankle. She forced it in, then tore it out, severing his Achille's tendon. Elliott hobbled a step or two and collapsed.

With no time to waste, Elspeth raced to the ladder, Elliott dragging himself along behind her as she hurtled down, taking two steps at a time, until her feet hit solid ground and she was off, running through the darkness, through the fireplace and out the wardrobe, the key clasped tightly in her fist.

She didn't stop, bursting onto the landing, down the stairs, the door getting closer by the second, and then she was in the hallway. Behind her, the door to the meat locker smashed off its hinges and Sebastian stomped his way out. Elspeth ran, Sebastian following, down the hall, down that far-too-long hall, his ponderous footsteps ringing in Elspeth's ears.

She slammed the key into the hole, rattling it, trying to get it to turn, to budge, to move, not daring to look over her shoulder at the rasping horror on her tail. The key turned, the door opening as Sebastian raked his nails down Elspeth's back, shredding her blouse and breaking the skin. Elspeth didn't notice, adrenaline firing through her like heroin. She snatched the key, shot through the gap and slammed the door behind her, jabbing the key back into the lock as the door rattled in its frame, Sebastian barrelling into it, the handle beginning to twist.

Elspeth turned the key and the lock snapped shut.

Sebastian pounded his fists against the door, shrieking uncontrollably, but it would do him no good. She was free. She was safe. Elspeth stumbled backwards, almost toppling down the porch stairs.

'I beat you! I beat you, motherfucker!' She cried, the wind blowing through her hair, blood running down her back. She stood, weirdly triumphant, the rain lashing her bruised and beaten body. She clenched her fists and screamed at the door.

'I fucking won!'

33

SHE BYPASSED HER OWN CAR, CARRYING ON TO AIDEN'S WHITE van. Her car keys were in her handbag, and her handbag was up *there*, never to be seen again.

It didn't matter.

She knew how irresponsible Aiden could be, so she climbed into the van and smiled at the keys dangling in the ignition. Her run of bad luck had come to an end.

She cried.

Hannah. Ted. Deek. Laura. Aiden. Robert. Gordon.

Dead, all dead, and for the sake of their ridiculous Mickey Mouse degree that wouldn't amount to shit in Aberdeen, or Scotland, or anywhere else for that matter. Four years wasted, seven lives lost.

And Mr Crawford too. That makes eight.

She considered going to the cliff and looking over, to see the wreckage of Crawford's car, then thought better of it. He might come climbing back up and drag her down to her watery doom.

I'd better get a fucking A for this, she thought, almost laughing, but not quite. She hadn't fully lost it. Not yet, anyway. She turned the keys, and the engine started first time.

Gordon. Oh Gordon, why did you have to come? Did Robert ask you? Is that more blood on his hands? He locked us in! If he hadn't, then at least three of us could have escaped.

She put the van in gear and drove, going nowhere in particular, just following the comfort of the headlights. She left Crawford Manor behind, the vast building growing smaller and smaller until the forest gobbled it up and the trees surrounded her once again.

That house of horrors...that damnable place!

So what now? She should go to the police. That was the obvious thing. All Elspeth wanted was to head home and climb into bed. Sandy would stir, and ask her what was wrong, but Elspeth would *shhh* her and embrace her, and together they would fall into a deep, dreamless sleep.

But she couldn't, not when she knew those creatures, those beasts, were still alive, contained within the Manor... and for how long? She thought of that attic, of the bodies that lay floor to ceiling, all those innocent lives lost to satisfy a savage craving, an insatiable bloodlust.

And to think Robert's uncle had allowed them to film there, with a mausoleum of insanity above their heads!

He must let them out after eight, to roam free. To play. To eat.

She shuddered.

The service station. She would head there. That was the nearest phone. She caught her reflection in the rear-view, her mouth and jaw caked in blood, black streaks of make-up staining her face. Her blouse was shredded, and she fidgeted, trying not to press her mutilated back against the seat.

She turned the wheel, edging round a corner, her beams picking out an abandoned vehicle. Gordon's Honda Civic.

Tears welled up again but she sniffed them away. She had to hold it together. Maybe he left his phone in the car? The sooner she called the police, the better.

Tell 'em to bring a few body bags too. A hundred should suffice.

She pulled up alongside the car and investigated, keeping the motor running and the lights on, anything to relieve this sinking feeling in the pit of her stomach. The Civic was locked.

See Aiden? That's how you leave a car unattended, not with the keys in the ignition.

She peered through the rain-streaked window, spotting a Dairy Milk Oreo bar on the passenger seat. God, how she wanted it. That bar was Sandy's favourite. Since she had quit smoking a year ago, Oreo bars had become her major vice. Sure, they both still drank, but just on the weekends. No, instead of the cigarettes, Sandy enjoyed a—

Her heart damn-near stopped.

'Oh Jesus...oh fuck no.' She wiped the rain from the window, trying to see in. That bag, that green handbag. It couldn't be. And yet it was. She recognised it. She knew it well.

After all, she had given it to Sandy for her birthday two months ago.

'Please no,' she muttered, her legs threatening to give up.

She staggered through the mud to the van and opened the rear doors, climbing in. It was pretty empty, most of their gear still in the storage room back at the manor. There were cardboard boxes, some flight cases, a couple of spare lights and tripods.

She grabbed one of the tripods, felt the weight. It would do the trick.

She jumped out into the storm, feet sinking into the mud, and slopped her way back to Gordon's car.

Hefting the tripod in the air, she swung it at the car window, a home run, the glass shattering. Elspeth reached in and took the bag, opened it, all the time hoping and praying that—

It slipped from her hands.

'No...no...'

Her legs buckled and she fell against the car, sinking down into the mud.

'Sandy.'

The rain continued to fall.

34

Sandy awoke in darkness, struggling to breathe.

Her head throbbed, pain needling its way across her face. Was she buried alive? She hitched in a sharp breath and shot her hands out, expecting to find wood or metal, a container six feet under the earth. Her prison.

Her coffin.

Instead, she met with a softer resistance, some sort of plastic. It stretched, her fingers probing, ripping it with her nails until light flooded in and blinded her. She shut her eyes and scratched at the black bag until she was free.

She was in a room. A cold, white room.

A room filled with corpses.

Her world shifted on its axis. She wanted to scream, but fear throttled the sound. She clutched her aching head instead.

It's a dream, it's a dream, it's a—

But she knew it wasn't.

What had happened? Where was she? Where Gordon, and that strange, sinister man? The last thing she remembered was the old bastard scrambling into the back seat, clutching a knife dripping with Gordon's blood, the boy's gurgling cries echoing in her ears. He had struck her with the handle, the light fading as he loomed over her, grim and unsmiling. He must have brought her here. Did he think she was dead?

Maybe I am.

Was this heaven? Or was it hell? Had her miserable old grandmother been right all along? '*Bloody lezzers go straight to hell,*' she had said, before Sandy had thrown a glass of water in her face and stormed away from the table, the perfect end to a typical Beaumont Christmas dinner.

It certainly felt more like hell. Bodies were strewn around, bits of them littering the floor; arms, legs, heads, and plenty of unidentifiable...*chunks.* Arterial spray decorated the walls. She staggered to her feet, her head woozy, gently touching her cheek. The pain in her eye was immense, and it felt like something (her cheekbone?) was broken.

No, she wasn't in hell. She was very much alive, and in a lot of danger. There were two more bin liners next to her, one sealed, the other torn open. What was inside had once been human. The skull was intact, but the flesh and muscle had been mauled, eaten away, right down to the stump of the neck. It wore a green checked shirt and Sandy knew it was Gordon, or at least it had been, once.

Now it was nothing.

But what about the other bag? She dug her nails in, tearing it apart, finding someone she didn't recognise, Claire Bruegel's lifeless face gazing at her over a mutilated throat.

Sandy fell backwards, struggling to breathe.

She had to get out of here.

Stumbling to her feet again, she made her way across the floor, sliding in the sloppy gore that coated the tiles.

She grabbed the cool metal of the handle and the door opened soundlessly. Leaving the meat locker, she found herself in an office. What was this place? Could it be Crawford Manor? Was Elspeth here?

No, no, no, she can't be.

She couldn't think that, not right now. She couldn't lose all she had to live for. Not Elspeth. Another doorway awaited, the door lying flat on the ground, wrenched from its fixings. It led into a corridor, one more room in this maddening labyrinth. She heard something down the hall.

It's just a man. Just an old man. You can beat him.

'Yeah,' she whispered. Last time he had the element of surprise, but this time she would be ready. She would smash his fucking brains in. A brass candlestick holder rested on a teak cabinet. Nice. It felt suitably weighty in her hands as she crept along the corridor, following the muffled noise from the other end of the hallway.

Someone was crying.

Another victim? Sandy looked left and saw the front door. It wasn't far. She could make it. If she ran, and avoided that massive pool of blood (who did *that* belong to?), she would be out in seconds.

But what if someone else was trapped, kidnapped by that old bastard and bagged up, left to rot in a roomful of cadavers? What if it was *Elspeth*? She had to check. She couldn't leave someone behind. So Sandy kept walking, clutching the candlestick holder, her head pounding. She came to a door and listened. Not this one. She kept going, trying the next door.

Not this one either.

Only one left. The low sobbing had stopped, replaced by someone humming a melancholy tune. A lullaby.

It sounded like a little girl.

Sandy checked back down the corridor and reached for the knob, turning it. The door opened and thousands of black, beady eyes stared at her from the darkness.

Dolls. Shelves and shelves of the things, and in the centre, a crib and a little wooden chair. A child's chair. In it sat a small girl with golden hair, facing away from Sandy.

'Hey,' said Sandy in hushed tones. The girl ignored her, continuing to hum her sweet, sad song. Sandy stepped inside. 'Hey little girl, come on. I'll get you out of here.' Her feet kicked a ball, and it rolled towards the chair, bouncing off the leg.

Still the girl did not stir.

Sandy took several measured steps towards her.

'Come on, we have to leave.'

She was close enough to touch her.

'We have to go before he finds out I'm missing.'

She placed her hand on the girl's shoulder and turned her round.

This time Sandy did scream. How could she not? The girl had no skin, her face a mass of thread-like veins crocheted across her skull, wet and dripping. Sandy backed up, horrified. She thought the girl was dead.

She was anything but.

The little girl — Harriet, once upon a time — stood, her slavering tongue licking across the stringy webs of her lips. She held the desiccated body of a baby in her arms, holding it out for Sandy to take. It slipped from her fingers and fell to the floor in a cloud of dust and the girl stepped on it, grinding the ancient bones to powder as she advanced on Sandy.

Sandy kept going backwards, shaking her head. Harriet smiled.

'No, no, please,' said Sandy, and then two enormous hands closed over her shoulders and her world went black.

35

ELSPETH TOOK THE TURNS FASTER THAN SHE SHOULD, HER foot pressed to the accelerator, her jaw set, teeth clenched, as she rode the mad ghost-train back to Crawford Manor.

It wasn't fair.

She had escaped once. Barely! She didn't know if she could do it again. Only one thing was certain — she had to try. Sandy was in there. Alone. She thought of that room, of that creature eating Gordon's face, and the two black bin bags beside him.

Oh god, she must have been in one of them! She had been right next to her all along!

Then she's dead already.

'No!' roared Elspeth as she navigated another hairpin bend. 'No, she's still alive. I know she is. I fucking know it!' The wheels of the van spun in the dirt, sending cascades of gravel and mud in a great tidal wave as she floored the pedal, the forest tapering off, Crawford Manor displayed on that cliff edge in all its infernal majesty. She took the last turn too fast and lost control, the van veering left and thumping down into the watery ditch, the airbag deploying into Elspeth's face. The jolt stunned her, and then she was off, throwing open the door and jumping out into the bracing deluge. She patted her thigh, the key nestled snugly in her pocket, and headed for Robert's car. Like the van, it was unlocked. Why not? There was no one around for miles.

Miles and miles and miles.

She opened the trunk, rifling through the contents. A tool box, bags of recycling, a can of WD40 and *there*, tucked away and wrapped in an oily blanket, was exactly what she was looking for.

The shotgun.

She unfolded the blanket and lifted the weapon reverently, cracking it open. That daft bastard Robert had been lying. It *was* loaded. Elspeth had rarely been so thankful for someone else's carelessness.

She had only ever fired a gun once, at her friend's farm. A simple game of clay pigeon shooting. She had two cartridges and missed with both shots.

This time, every shot had to count. She couldn't afford to miss.

She grabbed a torch from the toolbox and used a roll of electrical tape to affix it to the barrel. It made the weapon even heavier, but it freed up a hand.

The Manor was larger than she remembered, if that was possible. Elspeth walked up the steps, afraid that if she hesitated, that if she even *thought* about what she was doing, she would not be able to go through with it.

So many dead.

She shoved the key into the lock and turned it, pushing the door open, facing down that fucking hallway again. Was the shotgun ready to fire? Did she have to put the safety off or something, or was that handguns?

She supposed that when the time came, she would find out.

By then, it might be too late.

Fuck it. She closed the door behind her and held the shotgun up to her shoulder, her finger hovering over the trigger.

It's just like Time Crisis 3 in the arcade back home, or House of the Dead. Pull the trigger and BAM!

If only.

She strafed past the first open door, pausing for a second. Oh, if Sandy could see her now! She swallowed back tears. She *would* see her. They would be together again, the two of them. One day, they would look back on this and laugh.

Come on, let's not get hysterical.

The room was empty, and Elspeth carried on down the hall. The grandfather clock chimed. Elspeth waited, listening. One, two, three, four, five. Five o'clock. The sun would be up in a couple of hours. It was too long to wait. She reached the bear and checked both ways, the gun getting heavier by the second.

Run. Go. Sandy would understand.

'I can't leave her. I can't.'

She looked down. Red footprints led away from the room with the bodies. Elspeth crouched, inspecting them. Were they Sandy's? She knew Sandy's favourite food (chicken ramen), her worst fears (getting old and going blind), where her ticklish spot was (the back of her knees) and the smell of her farts (pretty standard), but she didn't know what the soles of her shoes looked like. Still, it proved one thing.

That someone else was alive, and they had left the room since Elspeth had been here.

It had to be Sandy!

First, she had to check the bags. She snuck into the office. Crawford's desk lay tipped over on its side, and the door to the meat locker was wide open, the light on. She crossed the threshold.

There was Gordon, or what was left of him. She looked away and inspected the bag next to him. There was a girl in it. A dead girl. But it wasn't Sandy. It was someone else, a stranger. Her throat had been slit, but she hadn't been eaten, not yet anyway.

That means Sandy's alive!

Calm down, you don't know that.

The warring factions in her head continued their heated debate, Elspeth opting out of the conversation. After a while, they stopped, but the silence was so oppressive, she wished they would resume. Leaving the room, she took a deep breath and followed the crimson footprints.

They led down the hall, past the entrance. Why hadn't Sandy tried the front door? Had she been panicking, confused, maybe chased? No, the prints were too close together. She had been walking slowly, stealthily. They faded, trailing off towards the last door. It sat half-open, inviting her in. What carnival of terror awaited her behind it? She hoisted the shotgun up, bracing herself, nudging the door with the barrel, her eyes narrowing, heart racing.

A noise shocked her, and for a single fleeting moment, Elspeth thought she was going mad, no, scratch that, had *gone* mad. Completely, stark-raving mad.

Music blared throughout the house at an apocalyptic volume, shrill violins shrieking a jaunty, old-fashioned tune, one that Elspeth dimly recalled from her childhood. It was from a Disney film, she thought. The vocals kicked in and it all came back to her.

Once Upon a Dream.

She couldn't remember which film, but it was an old one. You could tell by the archaic voices, a chorus of grand-mothers warbling away in church. But why was it playing *here*, why was it playing *now*?

Cold air pirouetted down Elspeth's spine.

She listened carefully. It was coming from upstairs. She moved the gun back and forth, the beam picking out the bottom of the staircase. Behind her, the door creaked fully open, the musical cacophony drowning out the sound. Elspeth walked, concentrating on nothing more than putting one foot in front of the other.

The song skipped, the needle caught in a groove.

'*Once upon a— Once upon a— Once upon a— Once...*'

She felt the trigger beneath her finger, cold and deadly, and thought of Sandy, stuffed into a bin bag and dumped in a roomful of corpses.

The music stopped as the needle was lifted and replaced. It was only off for a heartbeat, but in the brief silence Elspeth heard the patter of small feet. A child's feet. She turned to see a small skinless girl in a bridal gown racing towards her, an ancient curved scimitar clutched in her tiny red hands.

She raised it above her head and shrieked.

Elspeth didn't have time to think. She stumbled back-wards, tripping over the stair, and then the girl was upon her, slashing recklessly with the vicious blade. It nicked Elspeth's cheek, drawing blood, then ripped through the skin of her left arm as she raised it in defence. The music boomed above them as the little girl continued her frenzied attack. Elspeth reached out to grab her, but she was freak-ishly strong. Lights exploded in Elspeth's head as Harriet backhanded her across the face. She brought the blade down. Elspeth parried the blow, the scimitar embedding itself in the staircase, then reached up to the girl's face, grabbing a handful of veins and yanking them, twisting them until they burst, showering Elspeth with blood. It got in her eyes, in her mouth, as Harriet howled in agony. She fell back, still holding the knife, the long strands drooping from her face, leaking like so many garden hoses. She ran, choking and sobbing, and Elspeth grabbed the shotgun and gave chase.

The girl headed towards the front door, then at the last minute took a left. Elspeth followed, ignoring the pain in her arms and face, kicking open the library door. The girl was gone. A fire roared, the zoetrope embers flickering across the walls. Gripping the gun, Elspeth reached for the light switch and screamed as the scimitar pierced her wrist, impaling her to the wall.

Upstairs, the music continued to play. Elspeth aimed the gun with her free hand, searching for the little girl, a lightning bolt of agony flaring up her arm. She was stuck. She heard a strained thumping coming from the hallway and swung the torch that way, half-in and half-out of the library.

It was Elliott, dragging himself down the corridor, his useless foot trailing behind him. Elspeth took aim, her hand trembling. She closed one eye and tried to steady the weapon as Harriet burst from the shadows, flinging herself at Elspeth, clawing and scratching at her breasts and belly, her nails gouging out miniature chunks of flesh. Elspeth lashed out, swinging wildly, but she couldn't shake the deranged girl.

Thump, thump, thump, Elliott coming closer and closer, the music getting louder, Harriet shrieking like a banshee, Elspeth screaming, the fire roaring.

Her arm came loose, sliding down the curved blade as

Harriet snatched and tore at her, attacking her face now, going for her eyes.

Elliott was almost there, his flabby hands digging into the floorboards. Elspeth dropped the gun, closing her free hand around Harriet's neck, her fingers sinking between gaps in the veins like a handful of maggots. She pushed the girl away and bent over, slipping her arm down the scimitar, feeling it grind against her radius and ulna, then catching on the handle.

Elliott touched her leg, grabbing her jeans, and Elspeth yanked her hand from the wall with a sickening rip, shaking free of Elliott and lifting Harriet away from her, staggering forwards and holding the child aloft.

The child.

That's all she was, a little girl. An innocent. Could she be held responsible? Was a child accountable for their actions? Elspeth didn't give a shit. She hurled the girl through the air.

That little bitch.

Harriet landed in the fireplace, the old grey wedding dress bursting into flame, the inferno consuming her in seconds. She cried out as her arterial tubes popped and snapped, sprays of blood hissing around the room.

Elspeth felt the hands on her ankles again, pulling her, forcing her down. Elliott opened his mouth wide, his warped teeth snapping at her legs. The shotgun lay just out of reach. Elspeth jumped towards it, her fingertips grazing the wooden stock, as Elliott hauled her back again. She kicked him in the face, but he didn't flinch, didn't even notice. It was like he couldn't feel pain. She slid along the ground, catching him in the nose with her heel. Elliott lost his grip and Elspeth leapt forwards, her hand closing over the shotgun as Elliott used all his strength to heave her back towards him.

He climbed on top of her, pinning Elspeth's waist with his bulk and raising his fists.

Elspeth swung the shotgun round, aiming at Elliott's head. She thrust it forwards, into his gaping eye socket, the soft orb bursting as the barrel pressed against his skull.

She pulled the trigger.

Pieces of Elliott splattered the walls, chunks of brain-matter joining the still-writhing Harriet in the fire as fountains of blood cascaded from his neck. His arms went limp, falling to his side, before the great brute toppled onto Elspeth. She squirmed out from under him, holding her maimed arm to her chest.

The music stopped, then started again. *Once Upon a Dream,* for the fifth time in a row.

Once upon a fucking nightmare, more like.

She staggered over to the doorway, never looking back. She didn't want to see the mess she'd left behind, the naked headless mutant, or the little girl burning in the fireplace.

'I'm coming, Sandy,' she mumbled, as she tore off a strip of the blouse and tied it round her wrist wound. 'I'm coming, baby.'

She followed the music down the hall, heading for the staircase.

Back in the library, Harriet tumbled out of the fireplace, her clothes aflame. She crawled a step or two then collapsed, dead, by the sofa. The flames licked and spat, sparking uncontrollably.

Within minutes, the room was ablaze.

36

Sleeping Beauty.

Once Upon a Dream was the theme from _Sleeping Beauty_.

That was what Elspeth was thinking as she sneaked up the stairs, sticking close to the bannister, gun in hand. She had, what, one cartridge left? That was okay. There was only one more..._thing_ to deal with.

She hoped.

There could be more. A whole family, living in the attic, or the basement, or an underground cave network, or...

She thought of Sandy. Squeamish, easily frightened Sandy, who wouldn't watch horror films and who once told Elspeth she didn't like looking in the mirror in case there was someone standing behind her. Elspeth prayed to a god she had never believed in, asking that Sandy be okay, unharmed, and preferably unconscious throughout this whole ordeal. Elspeth would walk into the room where Sandy lay sleeping, a bruise on her forehead, the monster with his back to her, and she would aim the gun and blow the creature away and Sandy would wake up with a kiss and not know where she was and together they would leave this accursed place and drive to the police and—

It wouldn't be that easy. She knew it. Hell, Sandy was surely dead by now.

Stop it!

She was too late. Elspeth would have to live the rest of her short, miserable life knowing she had been unable to save her girlfriend, that she hadn't been fast enough, that she had even been in the *same fucking room* without realising. She had left her there, at the mercy of those people.

Left her to die.

No!

She reached the top of the stairs.

Her left hand throbbed mercilessly. No longer able to hold the barrel of the shotgun, she rested it on her forearm and swept the torch beam back and forth across the hallway like a searchlight. Listening closely, she identified where the music was coming from — right down at the end of the hall.

Well, of *course* it was.

She wondered if the brute had heard the shotgun blast.

Sebastian.

It seemed unlikely that he hadn't, impossible even, and yet—

Elspeth twirled one-hundred-and-eighty degrees, her beam coming to rest on nothing, except for some dust motes drifting lazily in the air like flies over a corpse. She turned back, expecting to see something standing before her, arm raised, scythe in hand. Again, she found nothing.

The corridor beckoned her onwards, and she accepted the invitation. Taking small steps, Elspeth walked, using the barred window in front of her as a focal point. She passed the first bedroom; the actors' room, where Laura and Aiden had died. She glanced in, saw the blood on the floor, the holes in the wall, and kept moving.

More doors. More bedrooms. She looked left, inspecting the wall just beyond the actors' room, noticing the way the partition changed here, where the door to Sebastian's bedroom had been bricked up and repainted. The faint outline of the old frame was visible under scrutiny. What other secrets did Crawford Manor clutch to its crumbling bosom? What dark and sinister figures roamed the hallways at night, what ghosts shuddered through walls and lurked in the shadows?

She moved her finger from the trigger. Any tighter and it would have gone off, leaving her defenceless. One cartridge. It was all that stood between her and Sandy. A bullet to the head. She felt hot, like the heating had unexpectedly kicked in, unaware that a fire was raging on the ground floor, consuming the antique furniture in the lounge. Nothing was sacred — the Steinway piano? Firewood. The medieval tapestry depicting King Arthur departing Camelot? Up in smoke. The fire burned, and no one in the house knew.

They soon would.

Elspeth continued down the hall. Two doors remained, one on either side. To the left was the bedroom where Aiden stored all the camera equipment and lights. She wondered — for the first time, surprisingly — how in the hell he had gotten into the wall. How, and also why? It must have been another passageway. The whole place was undoubtedly riddled with them, a maze within a maze. Aiden was probably using it to spy on Laura changing, that creep. She suddenly remembered hearing a noise when *she* had been changing in there too. Aiden? Or someone else, someone worse?

The end of the corridor. She checked the camera room,

the door wide open. It was empty of life. Steel flight-cases and bags of lenses and camera boxes lay scattered. She left them undisturbed and faced the last doorway. The music was insufferably loud now. Pale starlight from the window cast her shadow back down the hall, long and distorted. She could see the cliffs stretching for miles along the coastline, the waves lapping at the rocks, but no sign of civilisation, of help. Far away, a thin line of golden-red crested the horizon, the first glimpse of the morning sun.

Elspeth wiped sweat from her brow and steadied the gun. God, it was hot! She pointed the barrel and pushed it up against the door.

It opened.

She was not ready for what she would find.

37

IT WAS SURREAL, A CRAZED DREAM OF THE TERMINALLY INSANE. Despite the rising heat, her spine tingled. The room was large, and nearly empty. In the corner stood an aged gramophone in a mahogany cabinet, the music erupting from the weathered brass horn, and on the open dance floor the naked, hairy mutant waltzed across the room with Sandy, the petrified girl ensnared in his grip, her back to Elspeth. Her feet dragged lifelessly along the floorboards, but her head moved, pulling away from the grunting, snorting face of Sebastian.

She was still alive.

Sebastian's glassy, unseeing eyes swept over Elspeth, spittle dribbling down his drooping mouth onto Sandy's shoulder as Elspeth aimed the shotgun, trying to line up the perfect shot.

It was impossible. She thought back to the clay pigeon shooting, to how she had missed. She couldn't risk hitting Sandy. Sebastian's burly fingers hooked into her spine, drawing blood through her white shirt, lifting her from the ground. Elspeth followed his face with the beam, unable to think straight. How wide a spread did a shotgun have? She knew it was a cartridge and not a single bullet, which would have made it easier. Even if she aimed with unerring accuracy, there was still the chance she would hit her girlfriend.

If she could just get close enough to press the barrel to his head, take him by surprise. Or if she alerted Sandy, got her to shift her body out the way. But then what if Sandy saw her and cried out? Sebastian spun, Sandy's legs flying out from underneath her, and then she was hidden behind the bulk of Sebastian, the backs of his legs caked in blood and excrement.

Elspeth took a step towards them.

Over the noise of the record, Elspeth thought she heard Sandy crying out, begging, pleading. Elspeth's finger hovered over the trigger. She took another step. Sebastian spun again, whirling round to face Elspeth, Sandy's head lolling towards her. As if sensing her, she turned to face Elspeth.

Elspeth shook her head, tears running down her cheeks.

'No, no,' she muttered, tracing the tracks of blood that smeared across Sandy's face below the ghastly red hollows where her eyes once were, the fragile cords of her optic nerves dangling from mutilated sockets.

'You bastard,' whispered Elspeth.

She raised the gun.

She took one more step.

The song ended.

The floor creaked.

Sebastian's head snapped up, pointed right at her. He hurled Sandy towards Elspeth, her rag-doll body crashing into her, sending the two girls sprawling, the gun skittering from Elspeth's hands, and then Sebastian came for her. Elspeth dodged to the side, Sebastian's claws tearing into the soft flesh of her abdomen. She kicked out, knocking him off-balance.

'Sandy!' she cried.

'Ellie?'

A heavy paw struck Elspeth in the face, white-hot pain searing across her temples as lights danced before her eyes. Dazed, she shook her head to clear the cobwebs but Sebastian was on top of her, pinning her down, drooling over her, his rancid breath damp on her face. He held both her hands above her head in one massive, gnarled paw, and put the other to her cheek.

Then he leaned in close and sniffed at her, put her hair in his mouth and chewed.

'Sandy, help!'

'I can't see,' she whimpered, her fingers searching her face, brushing up against the dangling nerves. 'He took my eyes.' She sounded insane, her voice simple and child-like.

'Sandy, get the gun!'

Sebastian ran his withered tongue over Elspeth's face, up her cheek and around her eye sockets. She jammed her eyes shut to keep the probing organ out but he forced it in, licking her eyeball, sucking on it.

'He took my eyes,' sobbed Sandy.

'Sandy, please!' His hand was on her breast now, too hard, too tight. 'Get the gun!'

'Where is it?' Sandy crouched, sweeping her hands across the floor.

'To your left!'

Sebastian kissed her, the wet and sticky atrocity of a mouth closing over Elspeth's. She tried to turn away, but Sebastian was too strong.

'I can't find it! Elspeth, tell me where it is!'

Sebastian raised his head. Then, in a hideous, drunken slur, he cried out his mother's name.

'Elllllissshhhaaabetttthhhhh?'

Elspeth wriggled her head free. 'Left, left!'

Sandy did as instructed, groping wildly until her fingers closed over the weapon. 'I got it!'

Elspeth felt hands on her jeans, the nails scraping her belly, opening it. 'Shoot him!'

'I can't see!'

Sandy aimed the gun in the general direction of Elspeth's voice, but she was too high, too wide.

'Right a bit, right a bit, that's—'

A huge fist came down hard on Elspeth's face.

'Quiiiieeeeeet, Elllllissshhhaaabetttthhhhh,' snarled Sebastian, as Elspeth began to lose consciousness. She saw Sandy — two of her, in fact — holding the gun aloft.

She tried to speak but the pain in her face drove the words back down her throat.

As Sandy desperately called her name, screaming, Elspeth saw Sebastian leering at her, his hands caressing her body.

As her eyes closed, Sandy cried out one last time.

'Please Ellie, I love you, but you have to help me.'

I love you. The three sweetest words in the English language. It didn't sound like much, but it was enough for Elspeth's eyelids to flicker open. Seconds turned to hours as she reached up and placed her hands on the sides of Sebastian's head.

'Sebastian,' she said. 'Sebastian...stop.'

He tilted his monstrous head. 'Ellllllisssaabetttthhhh?'

Sandy tracked the sounds with the gun.

'Aim up,' said Elspeth through tears. Sandy complied. They both knew this was their one chance.

'Shoot him,' said Elspeth.

Sandy nodded. 'I love you,' she said.

'I love you too,' said Elspeth.

'Loooooove yoooooouuu, Ellllissshhhaaabetttthhhhh,' said Sebastian.

Sandy pulled the trigger.

38

SEBASTIAN ROCKETED BACKWARDS, HIS WEIGHT LIFTING FROM Elspeth's body and coming to rest in a crumpled mass on the floor.

Elspeth looked over at Sandy, at the bloody craters of her eyes. She still held the gun, pulling the trigger over and over again.

'Sandy,' croaked Elspeth, her ears ringing from the blast.

'Did...did I get him?'

Elspeth ran her eyes over Sebastian, smoke rising from his head, roughly half of which was missing. She took a moment to calm herself. 'Yeah, you got him.'

She crawled over to Sandy and held her hand. The frightened girl screamed.

'It's okay, it's me.'

Sandy turned her face towards her and Elspeth momentarily looked away in horror. Sandy's eyeballs had been clawed out, the skin around the sockets tattered and frayed. There would be no fixing it. Sandy would never see again. Elspeth took the gun from her and laid it down, then held her close.

'Oh god I thought I'd lost you,' said Elspeth.

'I came to find you.'

'I know. I know.' She ran her hand through Sandy's hair. Was that burning she could smell? She looked over at Sebastian. Him? No, it was stronger than that. Something was on fire.

The manor.

Oh shit.

'We'd better go.'

Elspeth staggered to her feet. She was bleeding from more places than she could count, but her nose was the worst. It was broken. Badly. Her vision swam in and out of focus. She held a hand out and saw two, staring at it, concentrating, narrowing her eyes until there was just one. She helped Sandy up and put her arm around her.

'Come on. The car's outside. Let's go home.'

'What about Gordon? He drove me here.'

Elspeth didn't respond, and Sandy understood. They stepped out into the hall, black smoke billowing throughout the house. 'Fuck,' said Elspeth.

'What's going on? Is something on fire?'

'The whole damn place is. Stay here, and lie down,' snapped Elspeth. Sandy lay flat on her stomach to avoid inhaling the noxious fumes as Elspeth raced to the bannister, keeping low. It was a nightmare. The entire hallway was ablaze, hungry flames devouring the ground floor. The hall leading to the front door was an impenetrable raging inferno. Elspeth recoiled from the heat, and dashed back to Sandy, skidding to a halt.

'We can't get out.'

'What about the windows?'

'They're all barred,' said Elspeth, her mind racing, trying to think, dammit, *think*.

'All of them?'

'Yeah. To stop those things getting out,' she replied, only half-listening.

'A back door?'

'No, we're on a cliff edge. There is no back door, unless you wanna jump two hundred feet into the sea.'

'Well *where* then?'

'I don't know!' Elspeth choked as the smoke invaded her lungs. She knew it could kill before the fire even reached them. 'Come on,' she said, staying low and taking Sandy's arm. She headed for the nearest door and slammed it behind them. The actors' room. They were safe in here for how long...minutes? Seconds?

'Is it bad?' asked Sandy.

'Yeah, real bad,' answered Elspeth, her mouth on autopilot. She picked up a lamp and smashed the window pane, Aiden's lifeless body still wedged in the wall beside her. Sandy screamed as the glass broke. 'Sorry, that was me,' said Elspeth, grabbing the bars and shaking them. It was no use. 'Shit!'

'Ellie, where are you? I can't find you.'

'I'm coming.' She grabbed a shirt from the costume pile and tore the cheap fabric into two strips, tying one around Sandy's mouth and nose, and one around her own. 'Try not to breathe in the smoke.'

'What are we gonna do?' Sandy was panicking, and Elspeth couldn't blame her.

Then she had an idea. The attic! But wait. No, now she remembered. The windows up there were also barred. There was no way out. They were trapped. All that effort, and for nothing. The house was a death trap. They were going to burn. She only hoped the smoke would get to them first.

The smoke.

The fucking *smoke*. That was it, that was the answer.

'I've got it!' yelled Elspeth, grabbing Sandy and pulling her towards the wardrobe that led to Sebastian's bedroom. It hadn't meant much at the time, but now it all came flooding back. The cool breeze as she had crawled through...

'Where are we going?'

'Trust me,' she said, crawling through the small gap and looking up, *way* up to where the stars twinkled above them. The chimney. She squinted, searching for bars at the top, but she could see none. Elspeth took Sandy's hands and put them on the walls. 'You're going to have to climb. It's a chimney, Sandy. It's our only way out.'

'Ellie, I can't do it. I can't see!'

'You have to! Or else we'll die here.' The ground beneath their feet was hot. Elspeth could feel it through the soles of her trainers. They were running out of time. 'You go first, and I'll be right behind you. It's brick, there're footholds all the way. Come on!'

'But what if I fall?'

'Then I'll catch you. You have to try. You have to.'

'Okay,' she replied in a small voice.

Elspeth thought of the horrors Sandy must have gone through already today and wanted to weep.

Her eyes. Her beautiful eyes.

Sandy began her ascent, unsure of her footing, searching for handholds. She pressed her back against the wall for balance.

'Come on, that's it, you're doing great,' said Elspeth, black fumes seeping into the actors' room. Soon it would billow through the chimney after them. Elspeth heard a door slam and her heart sped up. Sandy was about six feet above her and Elspeth jumped up, catching her heels on the brick walls. She used to climb up door frames like this as a kid, but she weighed a whole lot more now. She climbed, a human fly escaping the clutches of a spider. Then came the voice that froze her blood.

'*Elllllissssssaaaabeeettttthhhhhhh.*'

'What was that?' asked a fearful Sandy. She had stopped moving.

'Keep going,' urged Elspeth, catching up with her. 'It's not far, another fifteen feet.'

Elspeth looked down and saw a pale face staring back at her.

Sebastian.

'Jesus, he's here! Sandy, move, move!' screamed Elspeth. Below her, Sebastian was already climbing. How could he still be alive? Half his fucking head was missing! Why hadn't she properly checked his corpse? Ah, what difference would that have made? They had no more bullets. No more weapons. They were shit out of luck.

'Is he following?'

'He's right behind us! Hurry Sandy, for god's sake fucking hurry!'

Sebastian paused every so often to try to grab her. He was closing the gap, his gnarled fingers brushing her trainers.

'*Elllllliiiisssssssaaaabeeeeethhhhh.*'

'I can feel the wind,' shouted Sandy. 'I think I'm almost there.' Her feet scraped the wall and showered Elspeth with tiny stones. The floor gave way below Sebastian, collapsing into the blazing conflagration. He never even noticed, just kept climbing, one hand after the other, blood congealing around the massive hole in his head.

'Go!' shouted Elspeth.

One of Sebastian's meaty fingers snagged her jeans and

she wriggled out of his grasp, doubling her efforts, ignoring the pain in her hand and her arms and her nose and just about everywhere. She could feel spits of rain on her skin, smell the salty sea-air. Looking up, she saw Sandy at the top, her hands on the edge of the flue, and then she was pulling herself over. Elspeth's foot slipped and she dropped a few inches. Sebastian grabbed for her ankle, brushing past it, and she kicked him away, scrambling upwards. If he got a hand on her, it would be all over. Thick black plumes of smoke worked their way past her, obscuring Sebastian's wretched features. She scaled the chimney, putting everything she had into it, her final reserves of strength depleting fast. But she was *not* going to die today. Not after everything she'd gone through.

The entire manor moved. The walls buckled, tilting the building towards the cliffs.

'Ellie, what's happening?' shouted Sandy from somewhere on the roof.

Elspeth had no time to answer. She was too focused on getting out, and was almost there when Sebastian's clammy palm slapped shut on her ankle. She looked up and saw Sandy's face, her hand outstretched, hoping for Elspeth to reach out and grab her. Elspeth tried. She stretched, and for a fleeting moment their fingertips touched.

'Sandy!'

The building shifted again, flames roaring from the windows, ravaging the house. Soon, Crawford Manor and all within it would be razed to the ground.

Sebastian tugged on Elspeth's ankle and pulled her closer to him. Then he found the waist of her jeans and dragged her back even further until they were face to face. Loose bricks tumbled past her head as the flue collapsed. Any minute now it would come apart completely, and both

Elspeth and Sebastian would tumble into the mouth of the fire. The heat was unbearable. Sebastian clamped his arms around Elspeth in a hug.

'Elllllissssaaabethhhhh...miiiinnnneee,' he said, his face contorted into a grotesque smile. Elspeth reached out to the wall and her fingers found a loose brick. She yanked it out.

'My name,' she screamed, hoisting the brick above her head, 'is *Elspeth*!'

She brought it down hard on Sebastian's face and the remains of the skull cracked. She raised it again, smashing down, harder this time, the corner of the brick dislodging blackened stumps of teeth. Sebastian turned away, exposing the shotgun wound in his head, and Elspeth saw the pulsating grey brain matter inside. She closed her eyes and brought the brick down one last time.

The filthy bone fragmented as the brick rammed into Sebastian's brain like a fist through jelly. It splattered Elspeth's face and she dug her heels into the walls. Sebastian's head drooped, the pressure around her waist abating.

'Maaamaaa,' he sighed, before slipping away, down, down, down into the flames, and then he was gone forever.

This time Elspeth didn't wait. She climbed. It was easier now, the flue lying at a forty-five degree angle. Something touched her head and she screamed.

It can't be!

It wasn't. It was Sandy. Elspeth grabbed her hand, emerging from the chimney coated in soot, falling and rolling onto the tiled roof. She lost her footing, but Sandy held on tight, lifting her, pulling her, and then they were embracing, two women alone beneath the starry sky, as Crawford Manor groaned and a cacophony of voices from far below — the last surviving members of the Crawford brood — shrieked in hellish agony.

39

'WHAT NOW?'

Elspeth leaned against the crooked chimney, Sandy's head resting across her chest. Clouds of ashen smoke engulfed the building in a mass of smouldering toxic vapour.

Elspeth had already coughed up a lungful of black phlegm, and now she kissed the top of Sandy's head, just glad to hold her. 'I don't know. There's no way down.'

'Could we climb?'

Elspeth surveyed the wreckage of the roof. At least half of the attic ceiling had collapsed. The building had fallen again, the foundations tearing apart. A ferocious fiery chasm had opened between the two girls and the front of the building. There was no way across, only down into the blaze and certain death.

'We can't get to the front side. We just can't.'

'What about the back? Can we reach that?'

Elspeth looked into the vacant hollows of Sandy's eyes.

'Yeah,' she whispered. 'But it's on a cliff edge. About a hundred foot down, maybe two.'

Sandy tried to smile. 'You never were good with distances.'

Elspeth squeezed her hand, and they sat in silence for a while, the wood below them groaning and breaking as the all-consuming fire wrapped its flaming tendrils around the support beams.

'Someone has to see the smoke,' said Elspeth. 'They'll call the fire brigade, and they'll come and rescue us.'

'Yeah,' agreed Sandy.

'The sun's coming up.'

Sandy hugged her arms around Elspeth, too tight over her many wounds, but she didn't mind. She had fought her way through this house of horrors to rescue her best friend, her partner, her lover, and now they were here, together at last, one final time.

A little pain didn't matter. Sometimes a little pain makes you feel like you're alive.

'Tell me what it looks like.'

Elspeth thought for a moment. 'It's beautiful. Golden, y'know, like a sunrise on Christmas morning.'

'I know what you mean. I can see it, in my head. The light's rippling off the waves, so bright you almost have to look away.'

'Yeah. That's exactly what it's like.'

'Are we gonna die up here?'

The question took Elspeth off-guard. She paused, considering her answer carefully. 'Yeah,' she said. 'We're going to die.'

Sandy nodded. 'I thought so. I wish I could see, Ellie. Just for a second. To see you smile.'

'Not much to smile about,' said Elspeth, but she grinned as she did so. All she could think about was Robert Crawford's last film, *Burns Night*.

'Tonight, Robert Burns...in hell,' said Elspeth to herself.

'What did you say?' asked Sandy, giggling.

'I don't know.' She laughed, and Sandy joined in. 'I do not know.' They held each other. Far below, the interior of the building collapsed. It was only a matter of time now.

'Sun's up,' said Elspeth.

'Is it perfect?'

'It is. It's the most perfect thing I've ever seen.'

She was telling the truth.

'Ellie...will you marry me?'

Elspeth sat up and looked at Sandy, held her face in her hands, and kissed her deeply, passionately on the lips.

'Of course I will,' she said through tears.

Sandy smiled. 'I wish I'd brought the ring. It's at home in my sock drawer.' She felt Elspeth's face with her hands, caressing her smooth skin. 'I love you, Ellie. You're perfect to me, more so than any sunrise. You're my world.'

'I love you too, baby,' Elspeth said between sobs. A colossal crunch wrenched through Crawford Manor like an earthquake, as another main support disintegrated. The building rocked, edging closer to the cliff.

'Hey,' said Elspeth. 'If we stay here, we're gonna die, right?'

'Yeah.'

'And if we jump, we're *probably* gonna die. Right?'

'I guess so.'

Elspeth held Sandy's hand and looked out across the sea, the red sky reflecting over the water.

'You thinking what I'm thinking?'

'You said it's a long way down.'

'*Really* long.'

'And there're rocks at the bottom?'

'Massive ones. Gonna be hard to avoid them.'

Sandy nodded. 'Don't have much of a choice, do we?'

'No choice at all.'

Elspeth helped Sandy to her feet, positioning the blind girl on the edge of the blazing building. She waited, hoping for the flashing lights of emergency vehicles, for the blare of sirens. Somewhere between one-hundred and two-hundred feet below — Sandy was right, Elspeth was poor at judging distances — the waves pounded the jagged rocks. Elspeth and Sandy stood side-by-side, their fingers intertwined.

'What if one of us lives, but the other dies?' asked Sandy. Elspeth glanced down at the sea, then back up again.

'That's not likely.'

She squeezed Sandy's hand.

The sun hung low, turning the sky a brilliant orange, as if the whole world was on fire.

'On three, okay?'

'Yeah,' said Sandy, squeezing back. 'Just don't let go.'

'I'll never let go.'

Flames burst through the ceiling, licking the backs of their legs.

'*One.*'

The chimney crumbled behind them.

'*Two.*'

Elspeth took a last look at Sandy, then back to the morning sunrise. She didn't look down.

'*Three.*'

Hand in hand they stepped forwards, over the precipice, and then they were falling, down and down, their hands clasped, the wind rushing over their faces as they plummeted towards the sea.

Elspeth closed her eyes and found that she was smiling.

There was no fear in her heart.

Just love.

Pure, unconditional love.

AFTERWORD

I love a good slasher film. From the classics like *Halloween* and *Friday the 13th* to more obscure fare like *Final Exam* and *Body Count* and everything in between, there's something comforting about settling down to watch a bunch of obnoxious teens getting slaughtered.

It's the cinematic equivalent of a comfy pair of slippers, a genre that has been overworked to the point of saturation, and yet horror literature has a surprising dearth of honest-to-goodness slashers. I suppose the films are so disposable, with identical plots and little characterisation, that they often don't translate well to the page. After all, the selling points of many of these films were the grand guignol special effects and, of course, the boobs.

So many boobs.

If I'm beginning to sound like Robert Crawford here, I do apologise, but there's no getting away from it. Slasher films are trashy, but the best of them revel in that trashiness, and that's what I set out to do with *Night Shoot*.

Embrace the trash! Hey, whaddya know, I think I just found my new slogan.

I have to say, things turned out a little darker than anticipated, but that's just me, I guess. I certainly hope you enjoyed it.

Thanks once again to my wonderful wife Heather for all the support, and to Boris for being so sleepy and letting me write.

A big thank you to my parents, who read and enjoyed *The Forgotten Island*, despite me repeatedly asking them not to.

Thank you to Bradley and Sadie and Andy and John and Danielle for their feedback and encouragement.

And huge thanks to Connor for his wonderful artwork.

Lastly, my eternal gratitude to *you*, dear reader, for taking a chance on me. I will endeavour to never let you down.

～

This book was written to the following soundtracks —

Christoper Young - *The Dark Half*
Christopher Young - *The Fly II*
Christopher Young - *The Grudge*
Colin Towns - *Full Circle*
Elliot Goldenthal - *Pet Sematary*
Howard Shore - *The Fly*
Howard Shore - *The Silence of the Lambs*
Jerry Goldsmith - *Alien*
Jerry Goldsmith - *Poltergeist*
Jerry Goldsmith - *Total Recall*

ABOUT THE AUTHOR

David Sodergren lives in Scotland with his wife Heather and his best friend, Boris the Pug. Growing up, he was the kind of kid who collected rubber skeletons and lived for horror movies. Not much has changed since then.
His first novel, *The Forgotten Island*, was published in 2018.

Find David at the following locations -

 twitter.com/paperbacksnpugs
 instagram.com/paperbacksandpugs

COMING SOON

DEAD GIRL BLUES
THE NAVAJO NIGHTMARE (with Steve Stred)

Printed in Poland
by Amazon Fulfillment
Poland Sp. z o.o., Wrocław